NECROMANTICA

a novel
by Keith Blenman

For Crissy

THE ASH WOODS
A prologue

This forest knew life once.

Among the elder sequoias and babbling creek a village of elves had lived.

This forest knew laughter. It knew soft voices and gentle, tending hands.

Everything the elves had given was returned to them a hundred fold. The sparrows sang louder. The figs plumped sweeter. The trees themselves grew taller than any of their kind. They shaped themselves to the needs of their guests, bending into homes and forming a village of earthen souls.

For centuries the elves thrived. They raised their young. They studied the nature of life and developed magic around its principles. They were healers. They were harmonious keepers of the earth. They loved the land so deeply that it shared with them its name.

Hylorn

But that was a word the rest of the world was told to abandon.

"Forget the trees. Curse the elves. Do not speak of their ways- for their magic is twisted with sin and must be wiped clean from our lands."

Those were the thoughts of a human king- a man too content to a human mind.

His words soon became the cries of a kingdom.

A hundred speeches. A thousand declarations. In the end it was a single word that scorched this forest into oblivion.

"March."

Now there are no bugs to bite larger backs. There are no deer, foxes, or snakes to leave tracks in the dirt. And there are no elves to speak of or be spoken for. The ground is dry, barren, and brittle. Only the fossils of trees remain. Petrified, they stand shocked as rock pillars, twisted and misshapen. The homes they once formed remain as crooked, jagged cavities.

They have no leaves for shade.

The wind cannot rock their branches.

They stand as mere grey husks,

headstones to themselves and the lives they cradled.

This forest is haunted.

With all the life scorched away too deep for the souls to pass, they remain trapped in a fossilized mockery of their village. Too hurt to scream, too tortured to weep, and too scorned to pass away, the ghosts of this forest linger in silence.

The trees cannot recall warmth nor rain.

The animals are unable to stir, feed, or frolic.

The elves cannot rest.

All together the creatures of this forest remain pained and afraid from their final few moments.

Amongst their void, a single life approaches.

Every ghost becomes absorbed in his arrival. Every spirit lingers over his entirety as he sneaks through their vacant spaces. He is a human. Nothing magical, remarkable, or even noteworthy in a living woodland. And yet this place is dead. It hasn't felt life since the day the kingdom rained its magic fires. For the mortal's passing, the forest engrosses itself with his every step. It mesmerizes itself with his breath.

This human is tired. This human is frightened. But stubborn. He doesn't admit the fear to himself. He only feels its symptoms. His heart thumps hard. His skin perspires cool, slippery beads. His eyes leak warm tears that streak clean lines through the stubble on his face. His shoulder, back, and calf all bleed. Despite his pain, he struggles to maintain his pace. His stumbles are frequent and jagged. Exhaustion and paranoia are the pendulums swinging his steps. Several times he doubles back over his own dusty footprints –the only footprints- and poises a crossbow to the path from which he came. Several times he holds his breath and takes aim between the trees, waiting for something, anything to reveal itself.

But nothing does. Nothing will.

This forest would've relished in another's approach.

There is only the man; this human. And he grows weak. His breath is hoarse. His lungs scavenge at the dead air. The ghosts absorb his inhales and exhales like notes of their favorite lullabies. Those that breathed such ways in life wrestle for their memories of it. Whatever it is to pant, blow, gasp, or sigh, many of the cursed souls try to recall. Those that remember mouths absent-mindedly mimic the motions. They feel the way he pulls at the air from within, clutches it tight for just a moment, and then lets it fade like a forgotten love.

They feel the way his heart slows as he assures himself that he is alone.

They feel the way his eyes grow heavy while his arms sag.

He is tired yet continues to walk.

This forest feels his stubbornness. It understands determination as he staggers his way along the parched earth.

He is a rogue.

Every ghost sees him for the life he lives. From birth to this clumsy, blood trailing dusk. This man is a thief. He is a murderer. He is a fighter, toting worn weapons and tattered clothes. He is a stranger to this forest yet all the ghosts understand him as they would themselves. They absorb his past like bedtime stories. As a boy, his uncles pitted him against dogs. Sometimes for profit. Sometimes for sport. This forest knows how he escaped that life with hopes of a knighthood. It knows how his repeated thievery and constant mouthing off kept him from his dream.

Oh. Dreams.

The forest stirs over how his mind, even while afraid of pursuers, still manages to wander. It feels how he studies the veil of ash over its hard earth. It relearns itself through his glances into lopsided windows of tree trunks, worried over an imaginary ambush. He thinks of trolls, rangers, orcs, soldiers, dwarves, and even dragons. The forest, in all its years of life, had never once known dragons. To see one in his thoughts so clearly and with so much disdain is a glorious treat. The ghosts relish in how he maps out the ground, calculates places to hide, methods of attack, and how he might defend himself against any variety of opponents. The forest loves the way he notices shadows, corners, and climbing paths among the branches. It loves the feeling of his perspective on it, mirroring all the depth it had forgotten of itself.

This man is a strategist. He enjoys chess and card games but not gambling. He has a passion for music yet has only heard a handful of all the songs that ever existed. None of which had ever been sung in this forest.

The ghosts swoon over every note he knows. Some struggle to put them into order. Others try to reason why music was ever so important. Others still simply miss the way rhythms happen. They focus on his heartbeat and imagine a tune as it's reflected through his tactical mind with a natural talent for song that he himself will never be aware of.

The forest sees all of his crimes. It knows how he'd begun with fruit in markets and then coins from pockets. He took for himself. He took for those he knew. He had escaped many times. Other times he'd been captured. As a boy he liked prizes and souvenirs. As a man he grew to prefer the crimes. He liked picking fights against those larger and faster than himself. He didn't always win but he always got something he wanted.

As he walks through the forest all the spirits feel what it was like for him to take life. He felt guilty for the dogs but not his uncles. Never his family. The spirits crash against waves of his emotions. Deep seated tsunamis of fear, anger, and hardship. Between them they detect even a few small ripples of joy. But all the waves, the fervor, grow smaller as he ages. It was only just before he started killing for money that all his feelings stilled.

The ghosts who still know pity do pity him for this. He doesn't know the gravity of his actions. He doesn't understand the things he takes away. For all he's seen and done, he can't understand death like the forest.

He is a visitor.

The forest feels the way he begins to regard his surroundings. Exhausted as he is the dead trees and bare ground unsettle him awake. The flat gray of everything gives him discomfort. He concludes to know this place from stories and chatter. Discussion in pubs. The few words of the king he caught himself reading. He knows this place had once been Hylorn, but everything he knows with certainty is a lie. The forest wants to scream as it feels his version of its story. If only its ghosts could remember how.

The king had told his people of a growing evil. He told his subjects how the elves acted in death as sacrificial creatures who would steal their children and conjure darkness throughout the kingdom. They were twisting life in ways unnatural. They were trapping souls in bodies meant to die. They were heathens raising the dead. They were a festering evil against the king's great nation and grand gods. They would bring suffering, pain, and sin. And just like so many enemies of the pure kingdom, they were to be exterminated.

The forest feels how this man recalls the chatter as

he looks over its dead trees. It knows his discomfort by this place as he imagines its evil, snarling elves ripping the spines from babies and chipmunks in the name of black magic. This forest churns over his unrest and would give anything to remember what it was to ball a fist and punch his throat. This man, the first man, is first life the forest has seen in years, and he's unnerved by it. As though the forest hadn't already been hurt enough by the cruelty of mankind, now it must endure the judgment of this murderer's naivety. It feels horror based on fables he only ever half paid attention to.

And yet it can't hate him for this. He is only alive. He is only human. Such a small, unremarkable, and magnificent thing. It's not his fault for failing to understand.

It feels his contemplation. He knows this as a cursed place, and wagers on the idea that his pursuers won't dare enter. He looks to the darkening sky and sees stars speckling over the dead tree line. All of the ghosts remember the sensation of looking upon the stars. And what it means to be tired. And what a comfort it is to feel safe enough to sleep. The man is disturbed but knows the forest won't hurt him. He understands why his pursuers won't follow. They're more afraid than him. Maybe even guilty.

All of the ghosts collectively watch as he unfolds a scratchy cloth and several stakes from a pack. With the back of his crossbow he tries plunging the stakes into the earth. All of the forest hears the noise of wood clacking metal. It feels the man's frustration when the ground is too hard to be broken. All of the forest feels him fight the petrified soil and slowly give up. He grazes his hand along the earth, smoothing away the dusty layer of dead ashes, and look sharply up at the trees.

"It's warm?" he whispers. He speaks! He makes language with noise and breath! He communicates to himself –out loud– in such a way the ghosts had entirely forgotten. There is something so familiar and yet it's the most obscure thing they've ever witnessed. The words themselves gain gravity as he passes his hand along the ground, and then against the trees. Everything has a sensation to it. Rough, hard, and jagged. And every last bit is still warm from the magic flames of several years ago.

This forest feels the man's puzzlement. He looks at the trees, the ground, and the space between with new regard. He is in awe. He doesn't use his word noises as a caution against some overlooked pursuer that doesn't actually exist, but all of the forest catches his discontent as he ponders the place around him. It isn't right. He's certain of it. He's run from the armies that had marched through this forest. He knows they killed the elves and this place is meant to be thought of as cursed. He knows it'd been burned, and of the people who gave it a new name.

The Ash Woods

But this is wrong. He can feel it. The forest can feel him feeling it. It swoons over the question seeded in his mind. What elves would cast magic to destroy their homes and themselves? What spell could've petrified the land and erased all signs of life? The man is unable to reason it for himself. The forest feels his confusion and grows immense with gratitude. It watches him continue to walk as he touches all of the trees and grazes his fingertips against their surfaces. It feels his friction ridges. It admires his calluses.

The man steps into a dried out riverbed. He discovers soil soft enough to stake his tent. He's quick and haphazard with the task. He slides beneath the canvas, makes himself a small bed, and then patches his wounds before finally lying himself to rest.

As he drifts off to sleep he ponders the forest.
As he drifts off to sleep the forest ponders him.

PART
I

This humiliates me. Of course I understand the need for theatrics. The entire kingdom wishes to adorn pikes with our heads. Disguises are a necessity and your portion of the plan has carried us this far. Just as always. For your part you've never once lead me astray. You've never given me reason to pause or reconsider. But this disguise? With an inch short of a year to prepare this outfit is all you conceived of? Not that the breeze doesn't sooth, but Milady? This disguise? This?

Walking our horse along the open road, I can feel the passing eyes linger over me. Every elderly stranger. All the small children and crippled fools who stumble along opposite us meet me with wide-eyed glares and questioning glances. And all I can do to maintain dignity is keep my head forward, my back straight, and a hand rested warningly on the hilt of my sword. As you sit comfortably within the carriage, I muster all the energy of the great gods who carry our moons and bless our lives just to maintain the illusion that this attire is my normal.

It is quite the carriage by the by. The horse too is a magnificent specimen with its braided mane and chocolate coat. Sturdy and proud, whoever you stole the beast from must've truly loved it. Walking alongside this animal I can't help but feel feeble. While the horse and carriage gleam in the dewy morning sun, I sweat and stink. And all the world sees it. If any one prop will give away our nature I'm afraid it is myself. The horse and ride are infallible. Even in –especially in- this disguise I'm a platter of sin.

I should've been more open to my objections in prior days. But having never been one to question your mind, I uncomfortably obeyed. You had said, "I'll be a gypsy priestess from the southern mountains."

Standing in what I'd assumed to be undergarments, I had been foolish as always and quick to assumptions. "So I'll be a monk then? Or perhaps I can disguise myself as a Fortan soldier to be your escort?"

"Close," you had said with that cunning little smirk of yours. "Do keep thinking along the lines of an escort."

I hadn't understood.

You explained. Slowly, thoughtfully, you brought me to realize my new character. "Priests and shaman elves from the Folding Rock Mountains often indulge in rituals similar to those performed on the king before meeting council. They are serviced in such ways that pacify and bring clarity. You, to a priestess of the pure kingdom, would be regarded as property. No different than a utensil of sorts. Needless to say your presence in my life would be that of a servant."

"That shouldn't prove difficult," I'd said, somewhat perplexed. "I am and always will be your loyal servant." For the past eight years I've pledged to you my life. Although this had never been an official title, I've always felt clear in my status. You carried me through our escape. You gave me a second chance after the life I'd condemned myself to. I have always made clear that I am yours to do with as you wish. In my heart I can never see myself beside anyone else.

But even with that obvious truth half spoken you had made no sound. You simply grinned and brushed a lock of your raven hair to the side of your face. I didn't understand but felt there was no doubt some amount of mischief afoot. A bitter lump of hesitation grew in my throat. But I brought myself to swallow it down and asked, "What sort of servitude?"

And then you instructed me that undergarment I wore was the extent of my character. In private perhaps we would've both enjoyed its simplicity. At least I secretly hoped as much. But to wear it on the open road? As we pass caravan after caravan of weak and weathered travelers, I do my utmost to keep from feeling them paint their judgments over my bare body. I do hope you're amused. Hobbled men and beardless dwarves find themselves in chuckles. A small business of ferrelfs point and nudge each other to look. Oh and how I hear the whispered snickers of women. Never mind the robust laughter of children as they pass. "I can see his butt!" they say. They all say. Every last one of them. And oh yes. Yes, they most certainly can see my butt.

"Ho there!" calls a decrepit old hag on horseback. She trots from her caravan to meet us, toting a rusted lance in one hand and the reigns of a ragged mare in her other. She carries the weapon loose. I watch how sweat traces her wrinkles and sagging jowl. She is no threat and I have no need to treat her as such. She says, "You! Hooded man in the loincloth! Ho there!" and suddenly I'd very much like to treat her as an enemy. I don't though. I keep to our charade.

As the customs require I lower myself to one knee and bow my head, just as any seasoned *servant* would. From how you've instructed my actions, I act accordingly. "Good lady," I say, keeping my head low and not looking any higher than her dirt encrusted feet. The hood helps. Unfortunately for me it only covers my head and shoulders from the sun. You had told me something of its religious purpose. The human wearing it was no longer regarded a free man to the outside world. The hood may only be removed when the servant and priestess are alone. The rest of me remains exposed, except for those bits covered by the strategically placed flap of wolf skin. It seems I'm more trophy now than man. I would feel entirely naked if you hadn't permitted me to wear my belt and short swords.

"Whom do I address?" the hag asks, reining her horse.

I lie. In the kingdom of Fortia, admitting to the name Lama Percuor is a death sentence. Telling them the lady I travel with is none other the infamous necromancer, Mornia D'Onnyxa, would cause her to run screaming for protection. Amusing as that could be we must save ourselves for the real fight. I defer to our story. "My name is of no consequence," I tell the hag. "I am merely the loyal guardian and cabana boy of High Priestess Limilia Fortuna, speaker for the great sixth moon god, Shersher, and humble hand of Xevious, our great savior. May his veil be lifted and his strength guide us once again."

"May his veil be lifted," the hag repeats my prayer as we both bow our heads and pass an open palm over our own faces.

The ritual over, I stand on both feet again. I lift my head enough for the woman to see my face, but I keep my eyes low. "Milady is on the road to Dromn to seek the wisdom of-"

"Zerisk?" you yell from within the carriage. "Zerisk? Why have we stopped?"

"Forgive me, milady," I say, dropping to both knees and bowing my head toward the carriage. From the morning air I can feel my backside exposed directly at the hag. Never in my life have I truly appreciated the fine comforts of trousers until this day.

"Twas my fault, High Priestess," the old hag says, no doubt bowing her head in your direction. "I meant no harm but the road ahead is treacherous. I was uncertain if you are aware."

"Treacherous?" you yell. "Zerisk! Where hath you led us this time? Come thither and open my door!"

I dash to the side of the carriage and open its door, kneeling. From within you make no movement, except to gesture with your eyes that I should lower myself to the ground. It is all part of our ruse, but I'm certain you're most entertained. I do as you silently command, aligning myself with the doorway and dropping to all fours. I then feel your elfin feet step lightly onto my back. Although it is common for a priestess to use her servants as steps when entering and exiting transport, to stand on one is perhaps too commanding of a display. You certainly make the most of it. Resting the butt of your staff at the peak of my crevice is unexpected to say the least. I do my best to maintain composure.

"Forgive me, my child," you say to the hag in a far more patient tone than the one you use against me. "You say there is danger ahead?"

"Not so much ahead, good lady," the hag says and then points her lance to the West. "Danger is on route to intersect you. We only head toward it now because our road soon turns North to the Crystal Bay. We're fleeing to the Northern continent. Have you heard nothing of the fall of Bersmick, Calantra, and Brindenmire?"

You shake your head, which is a lie. The collapse of those towns is the reason we were heading for the capital city, Dromn, in the first place. But the old hag proceeds to inform us of the things we already know. She speaks of how the mining town of Bermisck stands, or rather stood, at the far edge of the Fortan kingdom. A place of untold wealth and riches, oft compared by humans to the bejeweled dwarf city Ara, it also had the unfortunate business of being located along the edge of orc territory. As a result, the town served as a key military outpost for the Fortan Kingdom. This of course led to some mild strife between the soldiers and civilian miners. Nothing that couldn't be settled without high taxes on the civilians striking it rich, which in turn allowed for generous pay to the soldiers who served the region. Although there had been some small squabbles and segregation between the two groups for years they were never of much importance. It wasn't until the past year that the miners finally grew fed up with the soldiers and began to take greater offense. In turn the soldiers became restless. Although no citizen of the kingdom knew how the riot began or who threw the first blow, the entire squabbling town had become a battlefield overnight.

Of course a number of orc scouts saw this as a compelling opportunity to expand their lands and devour some human flesh along the way. Who can blame them? So what began as a small riot escalated into a full-scale orc invasion. Several other towns and settlements fell before the kingdom had even known it was under attack. Instead of facing the orc army on open ground the king, former arch bishop Torquemada Stolzel, decided it was more strategically sound to use the mighty walls of Dromn to make their stand. All able bodied men were asked to stay and fight. Soldiers from every corner of the kingdom were called in as well. Of course when all the soldiers arrived the city became far too bloated for anything to be shared. The king decreed that all those who couldn't fight should flee for their own safety. "Can you imagine that?" the old hag says at the conclusion of her history lesson. "The largest, most fortified city in all the world, and the king orders his subjects to evacuate? I was uprooted from my home by a gang of thugs calling themselves loyal soldiers to the holy king. Uprooted by the very people sworn to protect me. 'Tis for the greater good,' they said as the largest of them rummaged through my cupboards, deciding which of my stores they'd keep and what food I was welcome to leave with. I had baked three fresh cakes the prior evening to lift the spirits of my grandchildren. Those were confiscated for morale."

"Good woman," you say with a shake of your head. "Xavious and the moons weep for your suffering. Although our great king no doubt acts with the intentions of the greater good, I can see how those beneath his grace acted as such. It is shameful indeed. Tell me more of your woes and I shall hold your restitution in my prayers."

"I am honored," the hag says. She becomes silent a moment, and as I peek up from my hood, I watch her gaze off into nothing in particular. "I have lived through the rule of four kings. Riminiuth and Bont Vichier were both good men. Riminiuth saw us through great plague and the years where mokata birds and dragons waged their wars in our skies. Vichier was stubborn and perhaps failed to hear his people during the long drought. But there was peace. Mine and my husband's woes were few. Then came the war monger, Yoffison. I do not mean to speak ill of any man before a priestess, good lady."

"Please," you say. "I will hear you through."

The hag looks to you with uncertainty in her eyes before she says, "He matters not. His chef saw to that. *The butcher met the blade*, as they say. We seldom think of how easily the few may change the fate of the world."

I lower my head. Light as you are, milady, the weight of you on my back begins to take its toll. I begin to think of stiffening my arms or at least giving my neck a good crack. But apart from the slightest droop of my head, I make no movement. I patiently remain on all fours with you on me and the woman leading herself into stories she's likely stored up in her mind for years.

"Kind King Stolzel was never fit to rule. He wields Yoffison's army like any other tune on that cursed violin he carries. I thought once of the peace to follow from appointing a holy man king. A man of Xavious should be just and yet, the witch hunts? The cleansing of the frontiers? Holy rule and dogmatic law. Most of my husband's earnings are taxed away under the guise that humbleness is the way of righteousness. Easy for the king to say from his new brass palace. Now the curfews and marital laws? Never mind those blasted citywide hymns every day. And it's only worse for the young. My grandchildren don't fear death like I had at their age. They fear life. They fear their own thoughts. The lessons they're given surely are not the will of Xavious. This cannot be the order of the world. For the greater good they claim. And my cost for that is only my home and risking my family on the open road during an orc invasion whilst the infantry sleep cozy in my bed. I suppose if the city stands after the war I will not be so troubled. Good king or no, Dromn has always been my home."

You finally step off my back and walk toward the hag. "You say every soldier in the kingdom stands in the walls of Dromn?"

The hag nods. "All those that still stand."

"Tis better news than I'd expected." You smile, more to yourself than the woman. You pet her horse on its side. Strands of its fur shed through your fingers. "Fear not, good woman. Think only of protecting your grandchildren. With every soldier there to save your city I have no doubt your home will be vacant soon. I will speak to my God and his brethren this night. I will pray the king be given a greater wisdom to guide this battle. I will pray the orc armies be defeated. And I will pray Fortia be given the rest it deserves."

Beneath my hood, I'm unable to stop myself from smirking over your words. The orc brood outnumber the Fortan army eleven to one. Although orcs have never been especially good fighters, they make up for their unseasoned flailing in pure numbers. With the battle about to ensue it seems unlikely the old woman will have a home left to return to.

"My thanks, your grace," the hag says. "Will you still travel to the city despite this news? If you like you're most welcome to join my caravan."

"I think not," you say. "Your offer is generous, but Zerisk is an able fighter and I require the knowledge of higher powers." In a manner of speaking, every word of that sentence is true, except my name of course. I am most certainly an able fighter. You are definitely seeking a higher power. You left out the details of breaking into the palace while the city is distracted by war in an effort to steal this higher power in the form of a trinket. But for the most part everything you say to the woman is honest.

"But High Priestess, the road to Dromn is almost certainly one of death," the old hag pleads.

And to this, you nod. You turn from the woman and climb back over me into the carriage. "I have little doubt of that, good woman," you say. "Little doubt of that indeed. Now, come Zerisk. We must make haste. I want to arrive in Dromn well before its expected guests."

"Yes, milady," I say. "With haste." Once you've seated I stand, wink to you, and shut the carriage door. The hag begins to turn her horse but I ask she delays for just another moment. I then go to the back of the carriage and open its rear compartment.

"Zerisk," you call from within. "Why have we not yet moved?"

"Just checking the gear, milady," I call back. I find a mokata feathered pack among our things, gaze fondly at it for a lingering moment, and then allow myself the nerve to part with it. "For you," I say to the hag, raising it to her in both hands. "Four short swords. I carry no more than two. They are light weapons. And fast. Should they be required your grandchildren will have little trouble wielding these blades."

The old hag stares at the pack before accepting it and resting it over her saddle. She nods and thanks me.

"If you make it to the port in Crystal Bay give them to an elf by the name of Ylrang Wind Catcher. He'll recognize the steel but if he doesn't tell them they're a gift from one dog to another. He'll understand. He will help you find passage across the ocean."

The old hag thanks me and asks, "Shall he hold the blades for you?"

"That won't be necessary," I sigh, staring at the pack and recalling the weight of the swords and how they'd whistle through every slice of the air. "They're payment for your voyage North. If milady's errand ends as we all predict I'll never have need of them again."

PART
II

Through the church's stain glass windows I hear the battle for Dromn underway. The orcs have breached the outer wall and are roaring through the streets, straight into the heart of the Fortan Kindgom. This is the world's most expansive city, often regarded as the glory of all civilization. Through colored glass and curved bars I watch as it begins to burn.

The calamity of battle echoes off the rafters. An ever constant clashing of weapons rattles the panes. Stomps from thousands of feet tremor the wooden floor. Screams are made by men and orcs alike. They bark out battle cries. They shriek over their deaths. Some sound oddly like seagulls and it gives me pause. I contemplate what other animals the ominous death rattles sound like. Goats. Monkeys. One bellow is vaguely camel-like. I assume it comes from an orc but can't say with any real certainty.

A human soldier yells a warning of approaching ogres with catapults. It's answered by the thunderous boom of a boulder blasting through the nearest building. Through the windows, I see red, gold, purple, and green refractions of a crumbling roof.

The church itself is silent. I sit in a pew with my arms outstretched along the crest rail, gazing at the magnificent flicker of lights, color, and shadow. There is something to the chaos outside I can't quite put a finger on. I'm mesmerized. Even a little humbled. For many of the soldiers in Dromn their world is a blink from its end. Tomorrow those who survive will ask each other where they were when Dromn either fell or was saved. Memorials will be erected. Songs will be written. Legends will be forged. But for tonight there is only chaos and death. Only the visceral things history will forget in its romanticisms. Tomorrow the world will begin moving on when the survivors drink to their fallen brothers. Tonight is the massacre that'll inspire the toasts.

The thought doesn't please me but I admire it just

the same.

It's getting late and soon I'll have to prepare. Not quite yet. The battle hasn't gone long enough for us to make our way deeper into the city. The sun hasn't set. I still have some time to enjoy the calamity and solitude.

From outside I hear a man's gruff voice. "Hold the line! They will not cross this line!" I ponder his rank and assume lieutenant. Higher command officers are always furthest back in Fortan formations. If he's defining territory he's most definitely at the front.

I see shadows sweep across the windows and smalls lights zipping above. I assume the flaming arrows are those volleyed from the orc army. It would seem foolish for Fortans to burn their own city to the ground. At least I wouldn't think they're quite so desperate yet. Regardless, the lightshow is quite dazzling through the colored glass. Quick comets of light blaze by. They flicker red, green, orange, white, and blue in the breadth of a heartbeat. Just as thunder follows lightning, the fiery arrows are accompanied by a rolling symphony of screams.

The windows themselves depict the life of the wizard messiah Xavious in every bold color of the rainbow. Among them, he's shown riding his dragon, leading the ascendants of man, and -the windows I'm most fixated upon- chanting over that ancient purple orb, *The Vecris*. The holy image on pristine glass streaks vibrantly at every passing flame. The shadows of warriors charge and slash their weapons beyond the still picture of outstretched hands open in worship. On the magical, mythical relic The Vecris blood spatters and then leisurely oozes down. The shadow of a man pierced in the throat by a fiery arrow thrashes around in a circle before tumbling over.

There are twelve windows in all, six on either side of the church. All of them extend from floor to ceiling. Between each stands an ornate statue of one moon god or another, and all of them are holding rounded amethysts.

The altar is centered between two podiums. At its rear are two gilded statues of Xavious bowed in prayer. Between them an enormous portrait carving of the king, Torquemada Stolzel, dominates the wall more so than any of the windows. He doesn't look as I've always imagined. I thought the king would be portly, balding, and perhaps with a slight hunch. In this image he's depicted as slender and clean-shaven with a thick frock of golden hair. He stands with his chest puffed proud and his hands occupied by a violin and its bow. The black crown he wears is adorned in a series of falcon claws gripping at his scalp. The talons of a single downward foot shields the bridge of his nose, and the dark lines of the ornament frame his face in a brutish sort of way. His hazel eyes have no atmosphere to them. They make his expression seem vacant in spite of a soft smile. When I ignore the darkness of the claws he looks docile, almost childlike. When I adjust to focus on the crown his smirk becomes twisted and sinister. Of course he's shown with bright rays emitting from nothing in particular behind him. And this makes sense to me. Royalty are always depicted as though they shit bursts of light.

Outside the church I hear that gruff lieutenant again. He belts, "For the king!" and is parroted by the voices of countless soldiers. *"For the king!"* they all squawk. The clashing of weapons intensifies. They're right outside. Between the statues of gods and their glass messiah I watch fragmented shadows fight, bleed, and one after another, fall. They all scream. Every last one of them screams until they can't.

"Do you hear that?" I say to King Stolzel's magnificent portrait. "Those men out there? They truly do love you. They fight in your name right up until their deaths. Not for the gods. Not the moons. *For the king.* You must be quite proud."

The portrait offers no response. It is a portrait.

It's drawing near time. I best prepare. I give my neck a couple cricks and stand. To the king's likeness I give my own sinister smirk and rid myself of that ridiculous loincloth. As I scratch and dress, I can't help but take delight in the solitude. All the horrors of war are festering outside these walls while the church itself remains vacated. The Fortan soldiers won't dare station themselves within the church, nor even allow for the fight to seep through its walls. Sacred ground is sacred ground. To spoil this holy flooring with orc blood is undoubtedly one type of sin or another. As for the orcs, I'm uncertain as to whether or not they're the sort to be burdened by religion. I know they too won't dare bring the fight into the church out of fear of provoking the gods of man. This in itself is mildly amusing. Stolzel, the good king himself, is also a man of the cloth. Prior to his reign he'd been an archbishop. The orcs won't dare deface holy ground and yet they're zealous in their effort to claim holy man's head.

Funny too, I think, refocusing on the image of the king, how those devoted to their gods always feel they can do more good once they're empowered. "I'd wager that's what you sell yourself," I say to the portrait. "Justification to every sin and the perfect explanation to your horrendous nature. *Think of the greatness I can accomplish for the gods while I am the most powerful man alive.*"

The portrait continues in its silence but I like to think the man represented would take my meaning. He might even attempt to refute it. Not that he'd make any new ground in his arguments. No man certain of his own purity and providence is worth listening to. This is unfortunate because often those are the very men most widely heard.

I tie on my bracers. They're made of hydra skin, which offers only light protection. But as I've lined them with throwing knives they make for a decent armor. The trick in battle is remembering which areas can be used as shields and which have been spent as swords. To the portrait I continue to ramble, "I've often wondered if you tell yourself it was the gods who encouraged you to murder the former king. Did you hear them, sire, somewhere in the back of your holy skull? Yossifin's death, as well as those of his kin began with that mysterious illness. But as his children and half the castle fell he somehow recovered. It was too well timed to coincide with your ambitions. Among reports of the king's health, I remember tales of you sitting at his bedside, playing an assortment of prayers on a lute. That is until you and the guards found him with a cleaver buried in his face. Milady and I used to argue whether you had bribed the royal guard and axed him yourself. I certainly thought so. But I suppose Mornia is right. Not a man of the moons. You couldn't risk anyone knowing the truth of your corruption. Especially not those you'd in time require for protection. More likely you hired someone such as I to do your dirty work. Yes, I see her point. It was a hired assassin. Maybe the chef who hanged for the crime but more likely someone else. That's a sin you could wash your hands of. All you did was tell some wretched fool the way to Yossifin's bedchamber. Perhaps where the guards would be and how you'd distract them with your holy presence. There's little wrong in some shared words, right?" I have to laugh over my little conspiracy theory. It's such an elaborate crime I've concocted for Stolzel and yet I can't see how anyone would think otherwise.

I adjust the belt on my trousers and tug at my short swords' sheaths. In part I suppose I regret giving that old woman my spare blades but I did keep the finest for myself. I'll need no others. These weapons were fashioned from spider silk, a gift from an eight-legged goliath whom we'd assisted some years ago. They're the lightest of my swords. A little too light. I hadn't used them for months upon receiving them, unwilling to trust their ability to stand against hard steel. To wield them feels like flailing paper. And yet once battle tested I discovered they'll slice straight through weaker metals. Orc weapons in particular. If there are any swords I trust to last the night it's these. If there are any I can expect to over exert my lunges with in the rapture of battle, it's these as well.

A few more knives fit into the slats of my boots. To the portrait I continue to ramble. "What of the wilds you sent your armies into? You deemed their quest a cleansing, did you not? I think it more a slaughter myself. The Torveskian dwarves. The wood elves of Hylorn. The Lomin tribes and most recently the dryads surrounding Jerbaisy. Villages of heretics throughout the kingdom, all of whom lived to their own traditions. And for it you massacred them all. I argue your gods are wretched indeed if their will is to do away with so many. I argue further, Sire, these conquests were not the will of any one deity. Let alone the lot of them. They were simply a demonstration of power. The unity of your kingdom, this grand empire you've constructed, is built on blood, fear, and man's willingness to embellish his own importance." Looking over my gear, I decide on my kit of lock picks, a length of rope, and then after a moment's thought, a couple more throwing knives. There is a war about and our own mission stands at the heart of it. The king's palace is at the far end of Dromn. As I wrap a black cloak of dragon wing over myself, I ponder the plan yet another time. Truthfully, it's not my best. But in my own defense who ever thought storming the castle was a good idea?

Well, orcs.

But we may very well succeed.

It starts with the king. Stolzel is a man of vanity. To illuminate this he keeps the kingdom's rarest and most valued treasures on display at the peak of the highest tower in his palace. The tower is so engorged with wealth that both sun and moonlight pouring through the windows cause the room to glow. At night it's said to be a warm beacon lighting all of Dromn. Most kings would perhaps favor a hidden vault or underground layer for such riches. But clearly Stolzel knows the power of flaunting his grandeur. Who among the peasants wouldn't look upon their king's palace and dream? What nation in the world wouldn't marvel at the tale of King Stolzel's treasure room? Regardless, with the orcs invading Dromn the entire army is focused on defending the city. Our mission is to reach the palace, gain entry, and make our way to the tower while the army within stares out the windows. Once there it's a single treasure we're after. An amulet by some ancient name you've mentioned to me a number of times. Its exact pronunciation I'm uncertain of and would only muddle in my meager human tongue. All I know is that it's shaped like Fortia's falcon claw insignia, and it somehow intensifies the powers of the wizard or enchanter who wields it. In the hands of a healer it could cure illness or mend even the most severe injuries in seconds. In the hands of a necromancer such as yourself... who knows?

Our path is simple enough. We'll sneak across rooftops as the battle rages through the streets. Once close enough to the palace we'll stow our gear and pretend to be innocent beggars too frightened to flee Dromn. They'll lower the gate or at least cast a rope for us to climb. Once inside we'll sneak behind the crowds and con our way to the tower.

My plan could afford a few passes on a whetstone. On the other hand, this sort of heist requires improvisation. An exact step by step is for the stubborn men who break when circumstances force them to bend. Simplicity keeps us in the wealth of options. Or at least that's what I sell myself as I check over my gear a final time. Truthfully our trajectory most likely ends in death.

"Well," I say to the portrait. "It appears I'm ready." I begin to turn, to leave. And yet the portrait compels me to stay. I've never been the sort for the lies of gods and man alike, but standing alone in their home, it occurs that perhaps a confession is appropriate. I'm uncertain as to what moon I was born under, and know few of the legends of Xavious. So I decide it's reasonable to explain myself to the portrait of the king. "I doubt the two of us will meet in person," I say. "But there is something you should know. I just- I wish you could understand that for the harm you caused me, I begrudge you nothing. You likely wouldn't recall, but once upon a time you signed and sealed my death sentence with your royal stamp. I resented this for some years but in retrospect I am a killer. For the safety of your subjects the order was a wise decision. Given the circumstances it may have even been your one good act as king. But I've not thought on it for quite some time. It's just- The thing that weighs on me," I trail off. Before I can continue I look at the doors and pews and make certain of my solitude. Reassured I turn back to the portrait and say in a more hushed tone, "Between the two of us -speaking one vile, unforgivable man to another- this caper is simply an expression of the heart. It may even be my one good act as a deviant. Although my companion has some different feelings on the matter I regard you with no more than a shrug of indifference. For all of your sins, you commited them because you believed in something greater than yourself. I am doing the same. You're a man who brought death to the outskirts of the kingdom. I'm simply returning it to your door. Your men are out there fighting, killing, and dying because they love you. I too am acting upon violence entirely for- For her. You found it best to take my life. She gave me a reason to live. For this- For my part in this caper, I want you to understand it has nothing to do with you and everything to do with her." The thought echoes and dwindles off into the same nothingness of its creation. I stare at the ever-silent portrait. For just this moment I feel honest. Even complete.

I then spoil the harmony for myself, throwing a knife from the folds of my cloak. The blade spins once and stabs the portrait square in the king's chest. "Of course if you shouldn't happen to survive the night I'll consider us even over my death sentence. I'll remember it as justice for your crimes against the world."

I run a couple steps up the wall to pluck my knife from the portrait. I then turn and move down the altar, heading for the bell tower where you're already waiting. I graze my fingers along the equipment I'm leaving behind.

Some of it had been so useful over the years. My collapsible dwarven crossbow. My assortment of exploding dragon lungs. Oh, and the *Werepenguin Beak of Ruin*. What a fantastic and powerful devise that proved to be. And with so many uses. Far more than some of the other items I've lugged around. One would think an invisibility handkerchief would've come in handy more often. Only once, and to hide a cantaloupe from you.

Moving on, I pass my hand over a vial of mokata blood. The goo is thought to ward off all living creatures yet never once worked as well as those gypsy grifters claimed. And then there's my travel stone. A little emerald capable of transporting its user to anywhere he wishes. Although thought to be immensely valuable it can unfortunately only be used once. This of course gives one the desire to save it for only the absolute most dire of situations. Even then there's no guarantee the thing will work. So if a scenario arises where I need the travel stone and it proves to be nothing more than an emerald not only will I die but I'll die a fool. I can't discard the thing because what if it does work and the day comes where I might require it? But what if I require it and it proves itself as nothing more than a pretty rock?

The debate over travel stones is the stuff of migraines. The result is that it remained in a pocket with an assortment of throwing knives for the past several years. However, seeing as we likely won't be surviving the night anyhow, I can't help but gaze at the little gem for a moment. I lift it from its mesh pocket and let it dangle on its necklace. I know I should part with the stone. I look over everything else and know it's best to leave it all behind. It's far too much to take along and I'll be an easier target it I try. If I die I'll never have need of it again. If I live I hope to never have want of it again. I gaze at the little gem and question if I have the stomach for the tales and toasts of tomorrow. There is only absolute doom outside these walls and even if we survive I don't know the sort of life that remains for me. I question if I'm a greater coward for accepting death or facing life.

It takes a moment to find my answer. I look to the portrait of the king, the statues of the gods, and the windows of their messiah. Before them all I put on the necklace. I tuck the travel stone beneath my cloak and armor and with a heavy heart leave everything else behind. With my newfound clarity I resume my walk to the bell tower, sigh, and then turn back to my gear to collect several more knives.

The night air is cool and crisp against my nose. It has a chilled scent. Well, chilled with an added hint of things on fire. Wood, flesh, and molten metals. It's dark outside. I pass some open windows and see only two of the moons rising over the mountains that guard Dromn. The stars are present and the taste of the air reminds me of the coming winter. Thankfully tonight is comfortably cool. This and the darkness of so few moons is appreciated, as both will be to our advantage. Cool air is good for running. Darkness is perfect for thievery. If not for the screaming and bloodshed below, I'd think it rather ideal.

I find you at the peak of the bell tower sitting on the ledge, staring at the violence in the streets. You're still dressed in your priestess robes, silently watching the battle as the breeze sifts through your endless black hair. Several neighborhood fires emit a red glow around you. It's been ages since I've stepped in this city, not since Yossifin's rule. I believe this is your first visit. Our clashes with Fortia since our escape from Jerbaisy have always been in the outer regions of the empire. Never the kingdom proper. They were small battles besides. Assassinations and robberies for enemies of the kingdom. Or simply for men with pockets deeper than ours. For all the notoriety we'd obtained in this city, it's an odd feeling to actually see it again. Especially with you sitting over it, good lady death quietly watching as the homes and soldiers of our greatest enemy are ravaged apart. One could think us revolutionaries for this night if we weren't only here for an amulet. Approaching behind you, I hold up my loincloth, let it get caught in the wind, and let it go. Your head turns slightly, regarding my presence with only your pointed ear. The loincloth drifts past you and you either watch it float away or continue enjoying the carnage below.

As an elf of Hylorn you know King Stolzel's ruthlessness better than most. Sure he's killed and fought plenty of our employers in the time we've been together. I know that anger. But it was during his conquesting years, the purification of Fortia, that his armies tore through your lands. From me he took friends. From you your family, friends, your homeland, and your entire way of life. A part of me longs to ask how those memories are affecting you. Looking out at the nearly endless landscape of brass lined, gilded buildings of man, it's a much further road into the city than out. If you're in any way hesitant over stealing this amulet, backing away now wouldn't be an error. At this distance, the highest tower of the palace stands as tall as the longest digit of my middle finger. Three story buildings near it are the same height as the notch between two digits. All along the way, pipes gleam the reflection of the treasure room's glow, which then glosses over every city street. For a moment I'm dazzled at how even the roads have a wealthy glaze to them. But soon I realize the glimmers of light are reflecting from the soldiers' armor. My heart sinks at the endless landscape of them, packed tight as bricks and leading all the way to the palace. Looking outside the city towards a star field of torchlight from the hordes of invading orc forces doesn't provide much comfort. But I don't have it in myself to ask if you're hesitating. If I do, you may read into my own anxieties. You may decide to back out or proceed without me. In my heart, I cannot have either.

As I ponder this a boulder flung from a catapult tears through the roof of the church just behind where we're sitting. The flooring shakes and for a second I fear the entire tower may collapse with us in it. It's enough to make me speak my thoughts aloud. "We could just return after the city's torn itself asunder. How badly do you want the umm- the thing?"

You continue watching the streets below. After a considerable breadth of silence and a small shrug you say, "Enough."

I can't help but smirk. That's all I have to know. So I stretch. I ready myself for our journey into the heart of the city. I unsheathe my short swords and give them a few quick spins to loosen my arms and get used to the weightlessness of spider silk. Ready and relaxed for a path of almost certain doom, I put up the hood of my cloak and offer my hand with the question, "Milady?"

As I help you stand, you tell me, "You don't have to come along for this. The amulet will provide you nothing."

And now it's my turn to shrug. "It's never the prize," I say. "It's all in the heist. The adventure ahead. And besides, if I didn't have you to get me into trouble, I'd get fat."

You smirk. Beneath the shadow of my hood, I grin like a boyish fool. Your smile always has such an effect on me. But it dies quick. Now's not the time.

You take another step toward the ledge and look out again over all the battle. "I suppose I should ready," you say. And then you pull the bow at the collar of your priestess robes. It unknots with ease, and you let the cloth slip free of your shoulders. The robe catches the night air and floats away, I imagine off to meet my loincloth at some nowhere in particular. You yourself remain, but not in your usual thieving attire. Still unfit for burglary, you're in a taut, sleeveless dress, as black as your hair and even similar in sheen. Slits on either side reveal nearly the entirety of your legs, adorned by bladed heel boots that extend well above your knees. Your ebony gloves mirror this design, extending from your fingers to beyond your elbows. When you glance over your shoulder, I can tell from the look in your emerald eyes that you're already expecting some comment.

The word that overwhelms my mind is gorgeous, but I gather my jaw and bury my first thought beneath another remark. "I feel underdressed," I say with a small flap of my cloak. "Are you expecting a dance as we storm the castle?"

"It's my big night," you say. "I'll finally have the amulet or I'll be dead come morning. Either way it felt like an occasion. I wanted to dress the part." You step down from the ledge and rummage through a nearby bag. First you remove a sheathed rapier and fasten it to the top of your boot. Without a belt in sight, I can only imagine the mythril strength of the garter that supports a sword in such a place. You pull from your bag two masks. You toss one to me and I watch as you put on yours. Like the rest of your outfit, it's black, covering only around your eyes with sleeves that fit over your elfin ears.

"A masquerade?" I ask. "I doubt disguises are necessary."

"I found these some months ago," You say, tying off the mask and draping your hair over the knot. "A lomin sold them to me. They're enchanted to reveal areas hidden in shadow. Mine also enhances hearing." You then kick your staff up into your hand and spin it around your back. How you're able to wield such a heavy weapon is beyond me. One end is adorned with a hefty, steel counterweight, functioning to balance out the enormous arbacapuch skull on the other. I think that's what the creature was called. Some dragon-like critter we bested outside the vault of a lord several years back. You say the skull provides its owner with protection. Looking at the horns and pointed teeth on the thing I'd say its power comes through pure intimidation. Even without the skull it's a massive weapon and even with your elfin grace you're but a twig of a woman. I'd even wager the staff has more girth than your ankles. Most definitely your wrists. And yet I've seen you wield the thing in battle and watched how it almost seems to dance in accordance to your will.

"Aren't you going to put on yours?" you ask, pointing at the mask still in my hands.

I look down at the slip of fabric with some skepticism. I've heard of many magics and through you have witnessed even the blackest of arts. But a mask that penetrates shadows? The idea sounds like the sort of tune any lomin gypsy would compose in an effort to make a sale. But to appease you I find the eyeholes and press the mask over my face. Sure enough, all of the night's shadows are softened. In the darkness of the streets below I see wounded soldiers doing their best to hide, rodents scampering along gutters, and other assorted disarray. The fires in the city seem to glow with additional vibrancy. And yet their light is less blinding. Looking at the thickest part of the battle around the church, I can the see finest scratches in soldiers' armor and scabs on the orcs' pocked skins. "What about my hearing?" I ask, realizing the mask doesn't have similar sleeves for my ears.

You step back to the ledge and say, "Quit talking so much. That'll help."

We make our way along rooftops. Quick leaps and light feet take us deeper into Dromn. You spot a pair of orc archers firing on approaching soldiers and slink your way toward them. I start to retrieve a knife from under my cloak but you hold out a hand, gesturing claim over the first kills of the night. Although I'm competitive and jealous, I enjoy watching you slip through the darkness toward them. Silent and graceful, you hop from one roof and catch the ledge of the next. You shimmy your way over, peeking occasionally to make sure of their position.

It's only the two and they're far too busy volleying arrows toward the Fortan army to take notice. I make note of how the soldiers marching in the street directly beneath them would make for easier targets. But if they fire on the nearby crowd, they'll be spotted and endangered. I've always thought the trouble with orcs came in quantity but perhaps they're not as foolish as I believed.

You make a humiliating display of the pair. As one readies his arrow you hook your staff around his elbow and against his back. You turn him like a lever, causing him to not only misfire but stumble toward his partner. The other archer spots you and in the surprise turns to fire his bow. What he doesn't notice is how you've caused his friend to stumble into his path. When he looses the arrow, it only goes a couple of inches before piercing through the eye of the first orc. It falls dead and a quick spin of your staff lands a flat blow against the other's throat. It gasps for breath as it collapses to its knees, and you're quick to take the bow straight from its hand, and then slower the quiver of arrows off its back. No mercy, I think. You want the orc to know it's defeated. You want it to die seeing its weapons claimed, its mind spinning with the death of his comrade. Still, it is a warrior and even unable to breathe, the creature gives an effort to stand and attack. Not that it gets far. Not that it ever stood a chance. You entertain yourself a little, spinning your staff into the air as you unsheathe your rapier, slice the orc's throat through a growing lump created from your previous hit, and then sheathe the weapon in time to catch your staff and knock the creature hard across its face. With its neck already cut, the impact of your staff rips open its throat. Rusty orc blood sprays everywhere. You somehow manage to sidestep the geyser and perform a small curtsy in my direction.

"Show off," I whisper, assuming you can hear me through the magic of your mask. I start to enquire over stealing its bow, or at least how you plan to carry yet another weapon, but a whistling sound cuts me short. I don't even see it, but reach out and grab the arrow before it can finish its flight for your head. I scan the direction it flew from and see the missile was fired from human hands. "My turn," I say, charging forward.

The look on the archer's face is one of bewilderment. His eyes widen. His lips part. He mustn't have noticed me when he fired because I can see his puzzlement as he shifts his gaze from you. As I leap off one building, I remind myself to thank you for the mask. But the thought is pushed aside as I roll onto the next roof. The archer readies another arrow, regaining his composure from the first shot. He's fast. I've only moved a couple of steps before he's pulled on the bow, staring me down, sighting me with the tip of an arrow. The tiniest glint of certainty comes to his expression as he fires his shot, sending his volley straight for my face.

I play with him. I can't help myself. As the arrow soars toward me, I angle my head away from it. Just enough. I feel the arrow pass between myself and the inner ridge of my cloak. It pierces straight through the back, whipping the hood off my head.

The archer's reaction goes from initial pride over the successful hit to immediate dread when he realizes I'm still coming. He scrambles for his quiver, notches an arrow and pulls on the bow. I keep my eyes trained on his as I make for another ledge. He fires again as I leap, and I appreciate the strategy. In the air, already set on a path, I can't duck out of the way or roll under his shot. He has me and we both know it. Except that as soon as he looses his arrow I throw a knife from my sleeve to intercept it. The two missiles spark against each other before spiraling harmlessly aside.

I land and continue my charge. I can see the archer's disbelief. He's wide eyed. Slack jawed. His face turns pale as he reaches back for his quiver, but I'm already too close. I unsheathe one of my swords and jump off a ledge, straight for his post. He brings the arrow over his shoulder, sliding the shaft along his bow. His eyes stay focused on me, and I can see the fear growing behind him. I can tell he's in wonder. Am I some monster? What magic must I possess to topple over him?

It's nothing really. I bring my sword up over my head as I soar towards him. I have no magic and use no trickery. I'm not the demon he sees in his final moment.

Just a man. Just as him. A mere mortal fighting for the thing I believe in. But between us I'm faster. I've fought through more battles and dodged more arrows than he could possibly know. I run my blade straight through his heart with the same ease I have a hundred men before him. He collapses and I roll forward, leaving my blade standing like a blooming flower stemmed from his chest.

Looking back, I see you mouth two words. "Show off."

We progress along the building tops for as far as they'll take us. Occasional archers and scouts get in our way but are taken down with ease. A beating here. A strangling there. One orc hisses at me like an asp. One human snarls like an orc. I make a small game of stealing the arrows from archers' own quivers and using them to rip holes in their sides. You're less subtle, twirling your staff like an angry wind as you concave skulls and knock men clear from their posts. We make morbid work of both armies, taking away all eyes above the fight and adding to the chaos below.

We reach a main street, one too large to leap our way across. Ducking behind a chimney, we watch a battalion of Fortan soldiers fortify one end of the block, form ranks and build a defensive formation. On the other end of the block a sizable force of orcs, goblins, and ogres are gathering. Both groups have lined soldiers to define their territory with a small skirmish of only a few between them. Both groups are cursing one another, calling threats, and screaming battle cries to antagonize their enemy's forward. And yet neither side is advancing. I don't know the city well enough to make any grand assumptions but I presume this point is one of strategic significance.

We survey the block, looking back and forth for a narrow point to cross, or perhaps a break we can creep through at street level. I consider a few ideas. We could join the fight here, posing to serve the king and attacking the orc army until we find a way back into the shadows.

Of course that takes us in the wrong direction. And if either of us are recognized or enough people question why we're wearing masks, we'll likely be attacked by both forces. The thought is less than ideal. We could continue traveling along the rooftops until we find a narrow crossing but looking around it seems this street goes quite a distance without any definitive end. Directly across from us however, the nearest roof has some brass piping extending out of it. The thing ends in a trumpet bell, and I have to take a moment to ponder its use. Gazing over the cityscape, I spot others like it. Some curve. Some protrude from the walls. Others end in several bells, all of which point down to the sidewalks. They're not chimneys, as those are consistently bulky stone not unlike the one we're crouched behind. They're certainly not plumbing but the thought of them being used as such gives me a small chuckle.

You whisper, "What is it?" and I shake my head. I'd be embarrassed to explain the image of these pipes ejecting feces onto the people and now's not the time. You seem to shrug off my most certainly odd expression and tell me to keep quiet. I nod. I try to make up for the laughter by producing my rope and pointing to the pipe across the way. I'm not certain you understand, so I gesture a walking motion with my fingers.

You scowl as I loosen the rope from its coil and whisper, "My boots have bladed heels. I'm stepping on knives and you want me to walk a tightrope?"

"Go overhand," I say. "Or wrap your knees." I pick a small selection of heavier knives from under my cloak and tie them around the handles, forming a crude grapple.

"And risk two armies staring up my dress?"

The thought of your garter forces me to swallow some daydreams. "You're the one who decided to wear that getup in the middle of a siege. Lovely as you are, this is the sort of risk involved. If both armies glimpse up your gown, well, you'll stop the whole war and I'll just go steal the amulet while they're stunned."

I hope for a blush but am given a roll of your eyes instead.

I tighten the grapple as best I can and throw it before you can give me reason not to. I can't help but take pride in how the rope catches the pipe and loops once around itself. Years and years of practice and my little trick never grows dull. I give the rope a tug to tighten the knot. Then another pull to test the strength of the pipe. It doesn't seem to wobble or break, so I tie the other end around the chimney. I step onto the rope and give it a small hop. It still feels secure enough so I whisper, "Just walk on your toes. You're an elf. When was the last time one of your kind ever tripped?"

I take a few steps out and then another hop to show you the stability of my makeshift bridge. Another couple of steps and I start to turn, gesturing for you to join me. But it's right then that the mortar of the chimney gives away. First the rope dips, and then I drop along with it. Unable to regain my footing, I continue to fall, catching the rope with one hand. In doing so, the rest of the chimney crumbles from my weight. All I can do is hang on and hope to swing safely into one of the windows across the way.

No such luck. I feel the rope tighten just above the street. It breaks my fall somewhat but not enough to prevent me from hitting the ground and skidding against it until the curb bounces me. I don't feel anything broken but as I stand I find it impossible to draw breath. I stumble and collapse onto my back, fighting for air. I writhe a moment, battling my winded lungs back to life. As I roll, I see you standing on the edge, readying an arrow. You angle your shot to my left, and I look in time to see an orc charging my way, raising his sword above his head. Your shot pierces through his arm and continues deep into his skull. He swivels in his step. His whole body goes limp and as he falls forward the sword escapes his grip and spins in an arc over my head. Finally I clamber a breath and regain composure.

I stand with weapons drawn. I'm ready for the next attacker. But it seems the skirmish has been delayed. Both armies are paused, weapons drawn, and eyes transfixed on their fallen guest. Me.

It's a funny thing I notice in myself. Even as a professional thief and part time assassin, I've never cared for silence. To be surrounded in it as battle rages ominously on in the city is perhaps the pinnacle of all discomforts. At least I'm no longer attired in a loincloth.

"Percour!" a man's gravel voice calls out from the Fortan's blockade. "I know this man! I know him!"

When I look to the human army I see the head of a man, three rows back in the crowd. "Luthro?" I sigh. He'd been a prison guard who had a habit of taunting me about a decade ago. His voice had been fuller then. I thought one of us had killed him. But then again it seems to be a night for being mistaken. I until just now also believed masks were able to conceal one's identity.

He sings out my name with an expected manner of disgust. "That man is Lama Percour, the murderer escapee revealed! He is the Fish Thief of Luna Falls! Our great king issued this man's death himself. Kill him! Strike him down with the orcs!"

Opposite this inconvenience, another voice booms out from the orc's blockade. The lower, louder voice. One that thunders like catapults. One that putrefies the taste of air and rattles all the windows. And of course it screams out my name. "Lama? Lama! Lama!" Why would it not?

I turn to this threat, first noticing an arm the size of me knocking seven orcs to the ground. An ogre, the most massive I've ever seen, breaks through the horde and stampedes toward me. How and why it knows my name is a mystery, although I have killed a small handful of its kind in my day. I don't doubt this matter is somehow related.

"Ha-ha! Get him ogre!" I hear Luthro call from the opposing crowd. "Shatter his bones!"

I spin my short swords to loosen my arms. I hope the flash of spider silk will slow the beast to some degree of hesitation but it's uninhibited. I yell out a cry of battle, but it falls short with a cough left over from my winded lungs. Still, I charge. Still I face the monster. I take several steps forward, raising my blades. As I near it, the creature swings its fist in a wide haymaker.

An arrow plunges into its arm. Then another through his eye. Another step and you land, driving your heels into its shoulders and the counterweight of your staff deep into its head. Like the orc before it, the ogre stumbles forward. I attempt a roll to the side and dodge its punch, but the beast's knuckle drops as it falls and smacks me across my face.

I see stars as I spin into the nearest wall.

You don't waste any time creating our defenses. Riding the ogre to the ground you empty your quiver into both the humans and orcs alike. Those who had been skirmishing between the blockades fall, most of them dead.

I lift myself onto all fours but the effort is more than it should be. I think to myself that I'm failing you. We've only made it halfway to the palace and already I've thrown us into the fight. A year of planning and all that work to get us this far and I've nearly killed myself twice in only the past minute. I'm done for. I know it. I gather my swords and drag them closer, ready for a final stand. Orcs and men from both blockades are charging for us and in my heart I swear I'll take them all before I let them close in on you.

I lift my head and try to ready myself for the fight. Dizzy over how much the fall and ogre took out of me all I can manage at the oncoming orcs is a threatening glare.

And it works?

All the orcs slow. Some of them collide into one another. All of them together freeze. For a second, I have to wonder just how horrible the bruise on my face must look. But then I feel a small spatter on my shoulder. I look up. The ogre you'd just slain is rising to its feet with you still on its shoulders. You spin your staff and the beast flexes its chest. You stretch your fingers and the ogre balls its fists, cracking its knuckles. Its tongue hangs out to the side. Its one eye glows faintly in its pupil while the other is a smear draining down its cheek. In the eyeball's place, the empty socket emits a glow instead. The ogre lumbers forward and a guttural groan escapes its throat. Its death rattle, used as a convenient enough warning for all who approach.

But the ogre isn't alone. Several other groans expel from a number of the dead around us in the street. Always from the ones who had been face down. You raise your arms, and dead humans and orcs alike pull themselves to their feet. Those nearest to the living waste no time in making an attack. Two soldiers are pierced by their fallen brethren. Several orcs are ripped apart by their own dead brood.

Luthro, still somewhere in the crowd, uses his opportunity to inform on the obvious. "Necromancer!" he screams. "Necromancer!"

It all happens in an instant but our battle is underway. Both armies break formation, clearly riled over their mysterious new enemy. For many there's nowhere to go but forward.

You spin your staff. You wave your arms. The dead respond to your magic. They do your killing for you. "Yes, that's right!" you yell, belittling both forces. "Face me! Fight me! Get yourselves killed! Become my soldiers! Grow my army!"

I try again to lift myself into the battle but am thwarted by the dead ogre's hand wrapping around me. "What are you doing?" I say. I cough.

"No, Lama," you say as the ogre lifts me, cradling me in its arm. "You're hurt. Regain yourself. This fight is mine."

PART
III

I never told you this, but my life was yours from the first moment I saw you.

How long ago was that? Eight years? Maybe nine?

I'd been in that dungeon for the better part of two years. Days and nights were rolling into an infinite stretch of nothing remarkable. I'd spent several days discussing my exploits as a thief to my cellmate, a rotten dwarf named Brugar. "I miss how the cherry blossoms would bloom above all else. Coupled with the smell of the ocean. Oh, and the green mountains! They're unlike anything I've ever known on the Southern continent. Can you even recall the last time we saw anything as beautiful as green? Even as a warrior nation, the Hyokians understand the delicacies of peace. Simplicity, intricacy, and beauty. They truly are a remarkable people. I do regret stealing that silverware and the ship, but after embarrassing the shogun and his daughter my options were limited. I'm sure you understand." I rambled on to Brugar over the lore of my life while lying on a decrepit straw mat, gazing into the darkness of our ceiling. "It's funny how little we've spoken all this time," I told him. "A word here. A threat there. But I never felt as though we had much to truly say to one another. Not until I killed you. Isn't that strange?"

I rolled to my side and looked at Brugar. He was still just as I'd left him, propped against the cell bars with his neck twisted to an impossible angle. His eyes were open but had finally rotted away, which was something of a comfort. For days they seemed to follow me wherever I went. Not that I had far to go. "I feel there's a connection between us," I told him. "A bond if you will. Perhaps it's different for dwarves but I'm quite excited. I took your life and for that I finally get to be done with mine." It was a simple matter. I'd already been locked away for the rest of my natural days. There was no hope. No escape. Just years upon years of sitting and waiting for time to finally give up on me. To make matters worse, they'd locked Brugar in with me. The loudest, most violent dwarf they could find. I'm certain it was just some form of punishment, if not a game or bit of fun. The moons know how Fortan men love their bits of fun. Every chamber in my part of the dungeon housed two cells. When they brought in Brugar the guards could've thrown him into the vacant cage next to mine. Instead they took amusement over us sharing. As did Brugar, I think. He'd made a quick point to turn me into a punching bag. He ate my food. He took over the straw pile I'd fashioned into a bed. He most recently took to attacking me out of boredom. We scrapped. We both took our wounds and, I think, regarded one another as equals. Not many men can hold their own against dwarves and I took his violent advances mostly as an opportunity to learn. For a brief period I grew to look forward to them. But as time wore on I grew broken, tired, and thin. The realization set in that this was all life would ever have to offer. So one morning I awoke Brugar with a kick to his throat.

He was quicker to recover than I'd expected and the struggle lasted a good while longer than I'd have liked. Long enough at least to change my stakes in the outcome. It's vague now but I remember losing the will to go through with it. I couldn't allow him, this animal of a dwarf to be the opponent that finally killed me. So a change of plans occurred while I clung to his back and he rammed me against the wall. And the cell bars. And then back into the bars several times more. Finally I grew committed to my will for victory and gave his head a hard twist. Her jerked forward, resisting the effort. The added tension only eased the kill. Another pull and he was given the escape that had been meant for me. From there it was a simple matter of waiting for the guards to make their rounds. Once they found us, or rather me sitting atop his corpse and picking my nails, I was given a thrashing. Shortly after the warden sent a letter to the king, requesting the death of a soul most rotten. And I remember how relieved I felt. I laughed even, although I couldn't fully explain why. It had been years since I'd felt so amused. They had to kill me. Had to. It was the only punishment they had left. I felt an added sense of victory in that Fortia was forced to shorten the terms of my confinement. Finally, I'd be given all I deserved. Finally, I had peace.

So there I was, spending my final days relaying to the corpse of a dwarf my story. I joked about all of life's little ironies. I rambled over the heists I'd performed and the battles I fought. Oh, the adventures I'd had. How I missed that thrill of danger and stepping into the unknown. But those days were gone. I had no family, no friends, and for most of my life I preferred the ease of such simplicity. Whatever time I had left would be spent in the motions of eating my final hidden scraps, sleeping, and defecating in the space between. "Who would've thought it?" I told Brugar. "The son of a slumlord and a four-breasted whore dies alone in a dungeon. Surely when they speak of my fate all the world will gasp and wonder what went wrong."

It was about then that you came into my life. From somewhere beyond my cell's chamber door, I heard a distant rapping and rustle. "Kill me!" the voice of a woman shrieked, barely a whisper through stone walls. "Just kill me!"

"Silence!" one of the guards said, followed by the distinct echo of a slap, several screams, and more calamity. I couldn't help but to lift my head and peer at the darkness at the foot of the door. It'd been so long since I'd heard a woman. I couldn't help but wonder at and doubt the sound. My breath held itself in. My heart grew still. The shrill screams and sounds of disaster grew louder than before. They pulled at me. I found myself half sitting, leaning, edging toward the chamber door. What mystery was this? Whose voice broke the stillness of my slow death?

The sound of a key turn jolted me with the most

fantastic terror.

"A visitor?" I thought or maybe whispered.

The door burst open. The whole ordeal must've taken but a few of seconds. From the chamber door to the other cell was a mere couple of strides. They could've had you locked in and left the room before I could draw a breath. And yet every time I recall the moment it lasts. It lingers for ages and days. Luthro was the first guard in. He'd kicked the door and held one of your arms. Another guard, some weasel named Birrit, held your other. Blood sprayed with his spit as he demanded your silence.

They held you face down. You thrashed your head around as you screamed for death; your raven black hair tossing wildly, casting waves at your every resisting motion.

A third guard followed. Lurch, I think he was. He held your bare legs together and fought to keep his footing. Of the three he was the only man wearing his helmet. I could never imagine how, but you must've caused the dent in its side.

All three men had been tattered with bruises and scrapes. I couldn't tell whether the blood streaks were from their wounds or yours. All of them struggled to hold you like they were hoping to contain a wild fire.

"By the moons be silent!" Birrit said as he brought his knee to your chin. The hit turned your head and as your hair was swept up I caught a glimpse of your pale, bruised face and the fresh cut on your lip. I remember noting the specks on your cheeks and being uncertain if they were from a spray of guard's blood or if you bore freckles. You turned your head back and as your hair dropped, it parted in an arch that revealed your pointed elfin ears.

You screamed thunder, loud enough I'm sure to startle the entire prison. I myself was lost in awe. A woman in the Jerbaisy dungeon. An elf in the Fortian Kingdom. Tiny, petite, and a match for even the guards of the strongest prison in all the lands. Pale, porcelain skin, and with hair like a weeping willow at midnight. What a radiant and rare maiden you were.

With all three of the king's men trapping you tight as a cross in their arms, they used all their combined strength to cast you into your cell. You bounced off the far wall just as the metal bars clanked shut. You rolled on the floor and cursed in your elfin language. I couldn't see the tears beneath your hair, but I knew the sound of weeping. You commanded them for death, and with you safely out of reach, the three guards let themselves have a laugh over your words.

"Or what?" Birrit said. "You're in our keep now, darling. The good king wishes you many moons under our roof. And most unfortunate for you the king's will is the infallible will of the gods. Enjoy these walls, rabbit ears. You'll be a thousand years older and mad before you see the outside of them." He smirked as he spoke. Even with a broken nose and a cut gushing red over his eye, he smirked.

You continued to threaten and Birrit continued to mock. I became distracted when Luthro turned to me and laughed in that hefty tone of his. "Lost a little weight there, Lama?" he said. "Thought we'd bring you a friend. Pretty little thing, that one. Least she was before we broke her face in. Gives you a good last look at all the twigging you won't do no more. We'll be feeding her too. Wouldn't want for you to miss the smells of the chef's gruel." He chuckled to himself. When I gave no response he kicked at my bars. "You got nothing to say for once? Where's the stupid wit?" He watched me a moment longer and then finally left with the other guards, locking the door behind him.

I didn't speak on our first day together. I just watched you scream, rattle the cage door, and plea for death. It took hours, maybe even a day or so, but eventually you cried yourself into a slumber.

I attempted sleep but was too excited and fitful for

rest. You had given such a fight. I kept thinking over the blood smears and spatters on you and the guards. And the dented armor on Lurch. Your wounds. Theirs. In my mind I kept trying to piece the battle together. How you must've fought. What it took to subdue you. Your scream. And oh the sound of your voice. I rolled around on my sides and back. I fluffed my straw mat. I paced my cell, and yes, watched you sleep. If I'd had a way to lay a blanket over you, or even one to provide, I think that may have calmed me. But without one, after all my restlessness, I sat in the corner of my cell with my heart pounding, watching as you slept at the gate of your cell, your hands still wrapped around the bars.

The next day you were hollering for food. But even then I think it was more to pester the guards than satisfy any other appetite. Few men crave food their first few days locked in a hole. That's when reality sets in and the belly ignores itself. But there you were. "I'm hungry!" you commanded. "You have to feed me! You don't keep prisoners just to let them die!"

I fought to break my silence. It was all too pleasant to hear a woman's voice so I allowed you your rebellion uninterrupted as I gazed into the eternity of my ceiling. It was always the blackest part of the room, so dark I could never quite tell where it began. It looked as a void would, lingering just overhead. Allowing me to become acquainted with it I suppose. The thought of food made it feel closer. But you were distracting me from its slow encroach with your screams and carrying on. It took some time but finally I worked up the nerve to strike a conversation. "That won't work, you know," I said.

You jumped back for the far wall with a noise that was somewhere between a squeak and a yelp. I hadn't meant to startle you but for having done so the consequences were immediate. I had attempted to tell you how they neglect the poorly behaved prisoners. Yelling, screaming, and fighting results in withholding meals, among other punishments. Thrashings more often than others. But you didn't allow me a word of it. As soon as my lips parted again I saw your sneer. I hesitated. Your expression was blood hungry. You looked at me the way other men and animals had in combat. You looked at me with all the venom of a striking viper. And just as I read your face I was being shoved against the cell bars and then thrown to the ground.

"Brugar?" I coughed, rolling away from the dwarf as he stomped for my head. I avoided several more attacks and even managed to land a kick into the side of his face. But that's when I realized his head was still cocked to an off angle. His eyes at that point were mush drained onto his face. And yet there was a faint glow in his sockets. Some distant light from miles upon miles away. I caught the sight for only an instant. Brugar kept coming. Wild punches and obvious attempts at latching onto me. He dragged one foot and stepped heavy with the other. His attacks were slow, weak, and amateur. Any sense of combat he'd had in life his corpse couldn't seem to recall. And yet my counters and strikes were all useless against him. He just kept coming.

Back then you still had a lot to learn. Brugar moved like a corpse. Stiff and deliberate. Had it been an open space, and had I not tripped over my waste bucket, he never would've caught me. Even starving and weak, I would've stayed a step ahead. But as fortune would have it I fell back onto the ground and his full weight was upon me. With his moistened, rotten hands he throttled me.

I didn't understand what was happening at the time. I was certain he remained a corpse, but I'd only ever heard of necromancy. I didn't know fully what it was or even how he was still able to attack. I just knew Brugar was after me. Dead or alive, he was back and ready to end me for his death. So with his wet hands preventing me from swallowing the air, I finally gave up the struggle and just watched the side of his vacant face.

"Do it," I mouthed. "I deserve this. Do it."

He pulled me closer, his fingers crushing down on my throat. Every instinct in me was fighting to breathe, wanting to attack Brugar, wanting to find some escape. But my will wouldn't stand another battle. To be strangled by my final victim was a fitting death. Something the gods of the moons might agree I deserved. I'd already bested the dwarf once. Now was his turn for victory. I let him kill me.

"Why aren't you fighting?" you asked while his lips moved somewhat in unison to your question.

That's how I made the connection. Brugar was dead. He wasn't any sort of undead and he hadn't returned for revenge. It was you. Brugar had merely become the instrument of your will. His body was your puppet. And after a moment his grip weakened, allowing me to draw breath.

You asked, "Don't you want to live?"

"Nothing," was the only word I could get out before breaking into a fit of coughs. The dead dwarf's grip loosened further, but not enough to let me free. I tried again to speak. "Nothing for me," was the phrase I managed to say. It was followed by, "Only rest. Please. End me."

It took another moment or day but eventually you released Brugar's grip. He collapsed back into being just a corpse. After I found the strength I rolled him from me. He'd become so decomposed that as I pushed him over his belly skin ripped and remnants of his intestines spilled out. "No!" I coughed. "You could've finished me."

"I don't get to die," you told me. "Why should you?"

I admit there was no argument. Instead I just collapsed and sucked in the tainted air, rich with his decay.

Later I felt compelled to risk talking again. I was hesitant but at best you'd speak back. Or perhaps decide to use Brugar to silence me. Either outcome would've been victorious. So I spoke my mind. "Why would they lock you in this Black? What could you have done?"

I awaited your answer. And waited. And slowly realized another outcome. One that crushed worse than Brugar's choking fingers. You were silent to me. I did my best to ignore the pang. I left the question to hang and shut my eyes. I joined you in the quiet.

Somewhere in the halls a guard patrolled, singing to himself one of the king's many hymns.

They brought food for you the next day. A runny bowl of gruel. One of the guards must've fancied you because with it was a spoon. You dashed across your cell for it, and in an instant you were heaping in spoonfuls without so much as chewing. "Oh gods," you turned your head away and gagged. "Oh gods. Human food. It's horrid." But after fighting a groan from your stomach, you scooped in several more bites.

"You'll grow accustomed," I said.

You jumped back. Brugar's body twitched on the ground, which caused me to jolt. Under more trusting circumstances, we likely would've laughed over the scare, but you just stared up at me from between your tangled locks and the bars joining our cages. After fighting down a couple more bites you said, "Where's yours?"

"Oh, I've already suffered my last meal," I said. "I killed our dwarven friend here so they've granted me a death sentence. Starving me to oblivion, as it were."

You scooped another spoonful of food. Slower this time. "They won't hang you? Or post you to the cross? Or run the guillotine through you?"

I sat up and moved closer to the bars. Not too close. You were actually speaking to me and as little as I tried to show to it, this was the most excitement I'd had in years. I didn't want to scare you. But to be spoken to again? Or rather, to be spoken to like an actual person and not as the bane of an overly territorial dwarf. I admit now the struggle to maintain some reserve was overwhelming.

"Afraid not. Lovely as those options sound, it's not my decision. Rather it's by rule of the king. Or the arch bishop. I'm still uncertain as to his title these days. In his wisdom he decided starving prisoners was the most humane among death sentences. The slow suffering is meant to prepare my soul for the eternal damnation it's about to face. I'm to use this time to realize all the pain I've caused and beg forgiveness. Beg to the walls, I suppose. The gods know moonlight never reaches here."

You stopped eating entirely and looked at the few remnants left in your bowl. "I was trained as a priestess and a healer," you told me. "If you wish forgiveness I will help you pray."

I grinned as a fool. It would be the first time of many on your account. Such an unexpected kindness from the elf girl who'd taken on an entire set of Fortan guards. And you were a priestess? A necromancer priestess? You were becoming more interesting by the second. And yet for such an overwhelming gesture I could only be myself. "That's quite an offer," I said. "But the gods never charmed my life before. I feel little need to interrupt them now."

"Oh," you said, continuing to look into your bowl. "Do you not feel guilty?"

"Not of everything," I shrugged and inched closer to the bars. "Not the killing. Not the plunder, or whatever things the good king says my soul will be penalized for."

You quizzically looked up at my response. You inched closer to the bars, peering around them and watching me as though you were sizing me up. To have you look upon me was every sort of uncomfortable. Under other circumstances I'd likely have run for the hills. I hadn't seen my reflection in years. For all my boasting to Brugar of the man I'd become I was still wasting away in a dungeon. I was nobody worth looking upon, and not even long for this world. I couldn't help but lean away and find somewhere, anywhere else to look. I felt awkward being watched and babbled something nonsensical like, "It serves little purpose. Begging for forgiveness when all I've ever done is give back what life handed me."

"Then," you started to say, but paused for a moment to look down at your bowl. "If you will not pray will you at least help me finish this rot?" When I looked up, you were sitting in your knees, holding your bowl up in both hands to the bars. Your head was down and your face hidden beneath the shadows of your hair. It was such a humbling moment. How could I refuse?

I looked down at your bowl and slowly reached for it through the bars. I said something foolish like, "Never again did I think I'd be punished with the chef's own gruel. I suppose damnation can wait another day."

Some time later, perhaps a few days, I was lying on my straw mat, staring up into the darkness of the ceiling again. It felt more distant than before. I wasn't sure if you were asleep or awake but I still asked what made you decide to feed me. In all truth I had to appear every kind of awful. The fact that I'd been squatting with a corpse for some time couldn't have helped matters. But you still did. You pushed me to live. And to this you said, "You seem like a kind man." But then you were quick to add, "But I suppose for all I know, you're some ruthless murderer."

My grin again was foolish. Idiotic. Perhaps even sheepish. "But I am a murderer," I said. "That's why I'm here. Or at least in part. The chase which led me here took more than a handful of lives."

You were silent for a moment before asking, "Soldiers then? Patrols?"

"The king's men, yes. Some hostages. A few souls who saw fit to stand in my way. Lives of those both innocent and guilty I'm sure."

"Oh," you said. "And what- Why were you being chased?"

"Why?" That truth I've always wished I'd kept to myself. "It started with a fish I suppose."

You didn't speak and I took your silence to mean I should continue.

"I'd been paid a handsome sum for the heads of several paladins. Having just completed my contract, I was fleeing, attempting to blend into a market crowd. My appetite struck me and I helped myself to a grilled trout on a skewer from some fisherman's booth. How could I have known he'd enchanted the food against theft? As soon as I bit into the fish it began to scream, announcing itself as stolen. So the fisherman took chase. Him I beat down. But he was a larger fellow and an able fighter. By the time I broke his knee the sheriff and his lot came running. I think also some people who fancied themselves as heroes. So I cut my way through the lot. From there I spent several weeks jumping between villages and woodlands, trying to outfox the Fortian army. My mistake, I think, was underestimating just how many soldiers the king had in the central kingdom. I'd make it to the outskirts only to discover a battalion already awaiting my arrival."

"Wait," you said. "I know this story. You mean to tell me you're The Fish Thief of Luna Falls?"

"You know me by that name as well?"

"The entire kingdom does."

Why my stomach grew a knot is difficult to say. I suppose I should've enjoyed the idea of an entire kingdom knowing of my exploits. But it wasn't so. To this defeating news of a legacy I sighed. "I thought it was only the guards who called me that."

"They tell your story of the screaming fish to frighten children and deter theft."

"I've been a killer since before I was a man. I'm told I'm the broken one. The man who deserves his death in a lonely cell. I've slain princes and dukes. I've stolen riches by the mountainful. I once cut my way through fifty three armed soldiers to deliver their commander news of his divorce. As requested. The letter pinned to his chest. With a lance. And this is how the world will know me?

The Fish Thief."

"Do you feel nothing then? For their deaths?"

I rolled to my side, feeling little need to lie. "No, I carry them. I think on them and wonder to myself sometimes, what would their lives have become had I not intervened. I'm not heartless. Without any pride I think you were right to say I'm a kind man. At least I don't feel evil in my heart. But I am a killer as well. Certainly more monstrous than *The Fish Thief* implies."

"You're proud of the death you caused?" you asked. "Do you regret stealing that fish? Causing so many men to die because of your actions?"

I was compelled to say otherwise out of fear I might offend you. And yet the words that came were, "No. No. I was born into a life of death. A snake doesn't feel sorry after eating a mouse. I'm simply saying I know what I am."

When I looked through the bars again you were standing against them, watching me. Your eyes were green.

PART
IV

An orc shrieks for her arms as they're ripped from her body. Her lepidote skin stretches until it snaps and she recoils from the corpse who pulled her apart. He fumbles with her limbs and then beats her down with them. Her screams are silenced. His dead, glowing eyes gaze off, seemingly oblivious to the horror he's just committed.

Men and monsters alike are shred to meaty lumps in display of your power. Cradled in the arm of a dead ogre, I watch as zombies slaughter our foes with your distinct flourish. You've always had a flare for theatrics in your manipulation of the dead. They block and parry like any trained soldiers. They motion to protect themselves. They play through the pain of being stabbed or bludgeoned. It's all for show. Soldiers, regardless of whether they be man, orc, or otherwise, have been trained to target vital points. Veins. The neck. The chest. Eyes. Weak points in armor. Regardless of kingdom, military training always revolves around the truth that their enemies will be alive. In the heat of battle, nobody stops to consider how your minions are able to take a hundred arrows without slowing down. A blade piercing their chests is no different than pelting them with rain. Chop off the hands and feet? That's another story. And it's one you've learned well to conceal. Your puppets react to their wounds. When run through, you release them from control and let them fall. One of your zombies has its guts spilled and you make it drop to its knees, casting an arm toward the moons as if to beg the question, "Why?" The glow from its eyes fades and it collapses back into oblivion. But it's all a charade. The soldiers think they've defeated a zombie so they keep their focus on those left standing. They fight your army like any familiar foe. For that you sometimes give them the upper hand. You give your opponents a goal and corral them into a direction. Just like I taught you; you never show your enemies what they're fighting until it's too late. You give them the illusion of victory. Let them step over the bodies of the slain. Let them fight their way closer. Bring them into your web of corpses. Then, just as they believe victory is at hand you spring the trap. Standing on the ogre, twirling your staff, you make the simple gesture of raising both arms. The faint glow of the dead eyes spreads like fireflies. Before the soldiers and orcs can even react, dozens of dead hands lift their blades. Men and monsters alike fall dead.

The show continues as some people pick themselves up and stagger back toward their ranks. They clutch themselves. Some struggle to hold in the bleeding. Their comrades rush in, chopping down at anything that might try to move. It's so heroic of them to race in after witnessing such terror. Also sad and perhaps even a bit comical that they would. Nobody survives your attacks, milady. Men rush in to save zombies only to become zombies themselves.

Fascinating as it is to watch you battle, the grotesqueness of it can wear on me. You're in rare form this evening and it shows through an excess of slippery carnage. I ask, "Must you strangle that man with the other's own viscera?"

"It's all for the audience," you say. "You taught me to use fear as a weapon. Tonight I'm their every nightmare."

Of that I have little doubt. You give all the standing soldiers reasons to hesitate. You fill them with terror and for it they spill easily on the battlefield. I admit some hypocrisy in wishing you would find alternatives to the method. Ones that aren't so violent against my own insides. Severed heads and stab wounds are one thing. Drowning men in each other's blood filled cavities though? I suppose I do have the luxury of being able to turn away. And yet I don't. I need to see this violence. I aided you, bringing you to this war. The storm of orcs besieging Dromn is but a drizzle on your wake. It was my plan that brought us here and for that I will not look away.

I remind myself that the orcs would devour all the wet chunks your zombies have slapped to the ground. The soldiers defending Fortia would gladly torture the both of us. They once celebrated my slow death. These men cheered for the annihilation of all the world unlike themselves. Together they spent years butchering families and villages. Their conquests slaughtered droves without so much as stern warnings. They cleansed their kingdom, leaving themselves as the only scabs left to be picked. Revolting as your work becomes, the sight of it trades but one bad dream for another. Make no mistake. My fascination with your skill outweighs the lurching of my stomach. They all had it coming.

Shocked as I am at your vigor, I can't help wonder over the sensation you feel manipulating the dead. Do you see through their eyes? Do you feel their injuries? Is there any part of them alive within? Is it like whispering to someplace deep in the minds of fallen soldiers? Or is the feeling more akin to flexing your fist?

Fresh meat from both sides close in and you return to previous tactics. Your zombie warriors fight like men. A dead man springs off the ground, kicking one soldier into the swinging axe of another. The corpse of an orc sends a volley of arrows back into the horde he'd charged in with.

Two dead orcs fight back to back. One tosses a knife to the other over his shoulder. The other catches it mid swing, slitting the throat of his opponent. He then turns around and throws the knife into the head of the first orc's attacker. I can't help but grin because you and I did the same thing once in a bar fight. It's the strangest thing to see it from here, milady. All around us soldiers from two clashing worlds are meeting horrid and gruesome deaths. In the midst of it all you've found a way to share with me a private joke.

For your wink I smile. Other sights keep me on edge.

The fight is pushing you to the brink of your powers. Not that you would admit to this, but I can see it in how your zombies fight. Their skill is beyond that of these common infantries, but through various subtleties I catch the crest of your abilities. One dead soldier stabs his opponent and then twists the blade before removing it. You would normally stab and twist in one motion. Not two. There's a dead orc who stands by hoisting himself to his knees. The first twenty had just flipped up or rolled into a stance. Some of your recruits are starting to fence with identical attack patterns. They're too spread out for either army to notice, but I do.

Even you, milady, have your limitations.

I push my way out of the ogres grasp enough to look up at you. And there you stand on the ogre's shoulders, spinning your staff with your eyes shut, deflecting arrows while slowly shifting your hips. It's as though you're dancing to some quiet rhythm that only you can hear. The glow from the empty sockets on your staff's skull adds a certain romanticism to the scene. In the night sky, it creates faint trails, looping wide arcs about you. Many of your enemies over the years have mistaken that glow as the source of your power. "Get her staff!" they always scream. "See how its eyes glow. Destroy the staff!" This amuses me because the creature's skull doesn't intensify your powers. It's simply dead and therefore reacting to your magic. The faint glow in its empty sockets marks it only as another weapon. It's just another one of your zombies.

In the ogre's arms, I'm still able to move enough to tear shreds off the bottom of my cloak. I tie off several wounds and shift my shoulders. I sting in a few places, but the stunned feeling from the ogre's knuckles has waned and I'm regaining confidence. I want to join the fight. I start to shimmy free, but feel the ogre tighten its grasp. You must've felt me squirming about.

It's bizarre you know; the thought of being safe in your dead ogre arms.

I look out to the battle and see how your corpse army is silently and obediently murdering everything around them. Some soldiers have seen enough carnage to realize the fight is futile. They're turning to run. The attacking orcs aren't nearly as bright, but they're not nearly as good of fighters either. I can tell you're only playing them. You're giving them reasons to panic. An occasional body still clutching its weapons will lash an arm up at those standing nearby. Some corpses will begin to move as though they're about to stand. The nearest orcs will attack these, but they're just more distractions. A quick movement of one corpse makes all of them look one way. You then raise another body to make the attack.

You steer the battle through the streets and I see the shimmer of the palace tower growing closer. Every step is one closer to your amulet. The gate is sealed with a regiment of soldiers blocking our path. I can see beyond them. Some windows and brickwork that should make for an easy climb. At least if we had a rope. I curse myself over not collecting what length of it I could. Still, it seems we're reaching to our goal. At least until some archer makes a lucky shot.

I scream when I hear the stick of an arrow above me. I can't tell where they hit you but know you've been struck. The ogre's arm loosens and its entire body begins to drop. All of your dead soldiers stumble. The ogre begins to fall and I roll away to save myself from being crushed. Looking back, you're falling, an orc arrow jutting from your shoulder. The ogre collapses beneath you, its arms reaching out as it drops. You land in the ogres hands and it hunches over you. Dozens of orc arrows stab into its back.

"No!" I yell, running straight for the orc army. I pass between your dead soldiers as they fall back to the ground. As they drop I unsheathe my swords and give all of Dromn a new enemy to tremble before.

I barely notice myself. The whisper of my blades is echoed by mists of blood. I liberate orc heads from their bodies. I slap the flat side of my swords against the arrows meant for me, deflecting them into other enemies. I break bones. I shatter faces. Their infantry surrounds me and I teach them to regret it. I become lost in my own rampage. One of them shot you. For that there are sliced torsos. There are severed jaws. And there are screams. So, so many horrible screams. But not nearly enough. At the far end of their horde, beyond these fountains of blood I spot several archers. I push the entire battle toward them.

I cut. I thrash. When a particularly brutish one stands over me I hack him through his knees before cleaving him down the middle. When an ogre approaches I leap for its belly and slash my way through.

Me bursting out of an orgre's back is enough to make the orcs wise up and attempt to flee. They run, cowering their way toward easier fights. But I'm not finished. The nearest one to turn its back on me is sliced open.

More heads.

More limbs.

When I'm finally to my goal, the nearest archer thinks he has me point blank, drawing back his bow. Before he fires I slice his weapon in half and then break the arrowhead off in my hand. I could've just used my swords but I gouge a hole in him with the very weapon he pointed at me. Not that it offers any satisfaction. Moments like that are for the enemy. Let them see their weapons fail. Let them see themselves humiliated. In the heat of battle I show them how weak they are. Perhaps I'm not as gruesome as you but I still teach them what it means to be a monster.

When the final archer starts to run I throw a sword into his shoulder. Yes, the same spot you were hit. He spins before landing in a roll and is only stopped because I'm over him, punching in a blind fury. He begs in orc tongue until I shatter his teeth. He struggles so I break his face. My knuckles bruise his skin before ripping it. The muscles snap off his bone and limply wiggle to every hit. My fist shatters his skull, cutting gashes into my knuckles. Even then I continue to beat my way through his pulpy brains.

It's not until his hand finally reaches up and grabs my wrist that I stop. I scream and try to attack for a moment, but it doesn't take long to realize it's a dead hand restraining my anger. When I relax, it loosens its grip. It then gestures for me to stand. I do and the arm falls limp.

I breathe a sigh of relief. You're okay.

I pick up my swords and flick the blood off of them. I note the sting of a few new cuts and scrapes but pay the pain little mind. The battle made me a little weary. For a second I let myself believe we're through the worst of it and all that's left is to collect your artifact in the tower. It's a pleasant daydream, but it only lingers until I turn around. Although my efforts scattered the orcs, I now face a hundred Fortan soldiers. They stand in rows with their weapons drawn. At the front of the battalion two men are holding you on your knees, twisting your arms. A mustached man with a lieutenant's feathered helm stands at the head of them, poising your own rapier at your throat.

"Well fought, rogue!" he says. "Brilliantly fought indeed."

I start walking toward him. I keep my head down, my blood soaked face cloaked beneath my hood. With the fires behind me and swords in my hands, the last thing they'll see is my eyes scanning over their ranks, planning the order in which I'll kill them. "Let. Her. Go!" I command.

The lieutenant chuckles as though the day is his. As if the entire city isn't a fiery war zone. I may have cleared the street, but plenty more orcs will soon fill the void. Still, he takes this little standoff as triumph and says, "I think not. Drop your weapons and perhaps I'll consider a fair trial. Turn around to keep putting your skills to use and perhaps we can forget your crimes entirely."

I do not drop my weapons. I continue my march toward the men. I retrace my steps over the slain and mutilated bodies of countless orcs. The ground squishes beneath my boots. "Let her go," I say. "If you know my crimes, you know how I'll make the pain last."

A hundred soldiers all chuckle. It seems my fight against the orcs wasn't enough to convince them. The lieutenant arches his arm. You wince. With this mask I can see blood trickle down your neck and into the bosom of your dress. It's a minor wound but it makes its point. I stop.

"That's right," the lieutenant says. "Any closer and I'll open her throat. Now drop your weapons."

It's not his words that convince me to lower my arms. I feel something brush against my heel. When I look down a dead orc's hand rises and gestures for me to stop. The orcs other hand squeezes a sword. All around me, every slain body is clutching a weapon. Those unarmed are slithering toward anything of use. Not their entire bodies. Just their arms. They make small, subtle movements. Ones I wouldn't notice in the middle of the night. Even beneath the mask I have to pay attention to observe their slow crawling. You must've been using the dead to gather weapons since I began my attack against the orcs. The bodies closest to the humans are all armed. Those closer to me are positioning themselves. I look to you. You look first to the lieutenant, then to me, and you wink. This fight is yours.

Every instinct tells me not to lower my swords. Even if you were able to control a hundred orcs, the entire battle could be lost at the flick of the lieutenant's wrist. But you've pulled us through worse and I give you your moment. Instead of charging forth for another merry slaughter, I play along. I give you an opening. "All right," I call out. "Please, just don't harm her." I hold out both swords in one hand, far out to my side. "I'm putting my weapons down," I say. I lower myself to one knee.

The lieutenant lowers the rapier and laughs. Truly, this is a proud moment for him. He tells his men, "If she moves, run her through." A few men behind you point their swords at your back. The lieutenant grins as he approaches me. "Don't look so defeated, rogue," he says.

"Look at all you've accomplished." He waves his arms over all the slain. "All of Dromn is under siege and the gods have granted me two champions to fight alongside my men." He puts the tip of your rapier under my chin. "Redemption for your sins," he says. "Yes. You sir. You will fight at the front lines, mincing the orcs as you do. But not too much. We all want your friend to have plenty of toys to play with." He then looks over his shoulder and says, "Men, you are to keep hold of the necromancer. She may wield the dead to fight for our cause. But should she turns her zombies on us, kill her. If this rogue tries anything peculiar, kill her and then him. We'll drive these sinners straight from our city, sweeping the orc mess out with them." All of the soldiers cheer. They've seen your powers and now they think to control them. The lieutenant whispers to me, "The gods always demand restitution. Win this war for me and I'll allow you to decide which of the two of you lives." You must've heard his ultimatum with your mask because it's during his whispers that you choose to strike. As the lieutenant turns to order his men I feel a gust of wind and hear the whoosh metal slicing air. All of the dead orcs throw their weapons at once. Swords, knives, rocks, axes, arrows, clubs, maces, and hammers are cast at the battalion. For just a moment, it rains an armory down on the Fortan army.

A hundred men are killed before I can blink. The few that survived wounded or in tact are cut down by their newly dead comrades.

I take a deep breath and stand. You do the same. Me with a hundred dead orcs added to my name. You with a hundred dead humans added to yours. Wasting little time you approach the lieutenant. Although he lives, a crude hatchet is buried in his shoulder. A sword and two knives protrude from his leg. Three and a half dead orcs are pinning him by the wrists and ankles. One of them pries your rapier from his hand and tosses it to you. You catch the sword at your side and flick it in his direction. The weapon nicks him right where he had cut you. He stares up at you, his lower lip trembling. You nod when your eyes meet. "This is the gods' restitution," you say. Then you open his throat. He gurgles and his heart handles the rest.

I come closer, tripping twice over the assorted bodies. Among them, I notice Luthro with a mace buried in the side of his head. I take a moment to consider just how far this battle has taken us and wonder how he'd survived for so long. The man must've cowered away from us the entire time, keeping himself just out of your reach. Not that it matters now. Nothing escapes death. Nothing escapes you. Still, this is the second time I've seen the man dead and it gives me some pause. I can't help myself but to kick at his side to see if he budges. When he doesn't I return my attention to you. The want to embrace you pangs at me. I nearly lost you twice in a matter of minutes, so the feeling is difficult to ignore. I know better though and restrain myself. If there were ever a time for romantics, it's far from now.

You sheathe your rapier and pick up your staff, twirling it twice around your self. A mist of blood sprays from the skull and counterweight, drizzling down on the bodies around us. Your attention is already on the same palace window I had my eye on earlier. "We're nearly there," you say, pointing toward the highest tower.

My compulsion subsided, I ask, "How fortified do you suppose it is in there? Surely someone saw us coming."

You stare for a moment. "Why aren't there any archers manning the walls? They should be showering us in arrows." We both take a moment to stare at all the empty windows and finally you conclude, "I suppose there's only one way to find out."

And that's all I need to hear. We bandage each other's wounds. The drumming sounds of battle come closer and I know we don't have long before this street is again filled with soldiers and orcs. "How do we get in?" I say.

"I'll handle it," you say. All around us bodies begin to lift themselves and crawl. My first thought is you're guiding them to smash through the front gate. Instead they move toward the nearest wall and begin collapsing onto one another. They clutch each other's wrists and ankles, snapping each other's bones and jerking their bodies into a structure. More corpses hoist each other onto the pile, grabbing hold and taking themselves into its form. It takes a moment of popping sockets and escaping death rattles but before long I see it. The bodies of the dead soldiers and orcs are joined together, forming a grand stairway complete with guardrails of severed limbs. Several more zombies ascend it and join themselves to the stairs and third story window.

Your dress, still too formal for its blood stains and battle tatters, flows with the night air as you ascend the first several steps. You look to me from over your shoulder and say, "Shall we?"

"Indeed, milady," I say, following you. "And I thank you for not making them a ladder."

PART
V

I lived by the grace of your charity. Well, your charity and the guards' indifference as to whether or not I survived the day. I'm certain they had our shared meals figured in a matter of weeks. And yet none made any action to stop us. The thought never occurred to me back then but over the years I've sometimes wondered if that was their intention to jail us together. To prolong my death perhaps? I've toiled that the effort was a manner of comforting their own souls from watching a man waste away before their eyes. But no. Perhaps not. They still belittled, beat, and tortured me with the same vigor as always. Their reviling alone corrupts the joke that they were men of conflicted souls. These were Stolzel's men. They were gatekeepers of the kingdom. Men charged with locking away Fortia's foulest sewage, safeguarding the people from the resurfacing of our muck. Truthfully I'll never know what kept them from stopping you. It may have been as simple as the chef prepared enough sludge for your bowl and they cared little over how it was spent. But I suppose it doesn't matter. When reflecting on those months it's mostly you I ponder. You, curled in the far corner, twitching and snarling –yes, snarling- at your dreams. Your thinning face. The darkening patches around your eyes. Those rings grew so dark that the little scar above your left cheek stood out like a tiny comet streaking your face. I know you tried to hide it beneath your hair but I always admired it through stolen glances. It's not so visible in recent years.

Watching you waste away over me was a humbling, troubled experience. For all the fight you gave when they first wrangled you in I doubted you could've bested a single guard within your second month of confinement. And all on account of some murderous whelp. The truth about myself is if we had met in an earlier time or another way I'd likely have slaughtered you for a few coins. Or hurt you for looking at me in some disagreeable way. I didn't deserve the slop you fed me. I most definitely didn't deserve to share your bowl. Your kindness, milady, was just as heartbreaking as it was beautiful.

We were cold. Always hungry. I'd have said you could quit feeding me to save yourself but I took each day for the gift it was. With rancid meat gruel and the stomach knots that followed, you kept me suffering. You lavished me with life. In our own private Black you let me endure the misery with you. If I died or we'd been handed a cellmate who knows what madness might've followed. Thankfully in the outside world the good King Stolzel and his men were enjoying their campaign of butchering undesirables by the village full. Half the kingdom flourished in its newfound purity. Those unwelcome were eviscerated in the apocalypse. Few were the days of new prisoners being marched through the halls. On occasion we'd hear some evidence of men not among the guard. A chain rattle one week. A muffled scream the next. The world outside our chamber slipped softly away. We had The Black to ourselves. So we'd ramble. We'd flirt and tease. We'd take an occasional beating or random threat from the bored security. Reflecting over those early days I would never claim to miss the dank and fleshy odors. Nor the grime crusting over my bars. But I was fonder of the world when it comprised solely of us.

For the longest time you wouldn't discuss yourself. At best you'd make small anecdotes or allusions to greater things. But in terms of your past and yourself you seldom revealed any certain truth. Not that I blamed you for keeping your story under lock and key. I was a convicted killer sharing a cell with the bones of my final victim. Not exactly the sort of human you divulge your life to. And, oh how you hated humans anyway.

"I just want to kill them, and then make them all stand up," you said in a vengeful, little rant. "And kill them all again."

In those early months I'd made a point to keep my hair over my ears.

I did eventually discover why you'd been thrown into a dungeon. After a few weeks of conversing you told me that you'd been caught trying to steal.

"Muggers and pickpockets don't land themselves in here," I said. "To call these cells home you've done deeds most sinister."

"I killed two soldiers," you said.

"You were stealing from the army?"

"Not exactly," you said. "The king. He wasn't there. But it was a caravan hauling his newly claimed wealth. I tried to get away with one of the wagons but there were too many. I can only manipulate a few dead at a time. The soldiers overpowered me."

Do you remember that, I wonder? Back when you could only handle a handful of clumsy corpses? All those years of training and practice and now you're unstoppable. But back then it wasn't even a thought. I was more intrigued in that it didn't sound as though you were stealing for the sake of theft. "If you were after riches there are hundreds of wealthy targets easier to plunder than the king."

"I know," you said and then tried to follow with a lie. "I just thought a carriage from the king's own wealth would be-"

"What were you really after?" I asked. You didn't speak after my interruption so I speculated. "Nobody goes from priestess to notorious criminal without the reward being worth the risk. Gold can be got at any street corner for one with light enough fingers and you being an elf in the world of man have hands lighter than most. Being an elf too, milady, and do forgive me if I speak out of turn, but the pursuit of riches seems petty for your race. You were after something more. Wealth for your kind comes in more priceless and unique forms. Not any coin would do. You wanted the one minted in myth. You were in pursuit of something grand."

You let my assumptions linger. Minutes passed.

Too many. I began to wonder if I'd overstepped myself, feeling a choke of insecurity just before you cleared the air. You said, "Six months ago the king ordered the village Dahlia exterminated on account of their eating shelled creatures. There was this old sorcerer who died in the massacre. Not a true wizard. But he was at least a child of the ancients. It was said he had in his possession an amulet that enhanced his natural craft. Supposedly without it he could make it rain at will. With it he was able to recreate all four seasons. In his younger days he could tell lightning to strike with the precision of threading a needle. But over the centuries his age deranged him. Along with his memories he forgot his magic. It's the only reason Fortia won the battle. Must've been. And in their victory the amulet passed to be wasted on a king. A mere human who could never wield it."

I leaned forward, listening to your story. "You say you can manipulate a few dead at once? So with it…" I trailed off, letting the possibilities brew, trying not to allow my imagination to boil over. "And you risked everything to gain it." I thought of the day you came to our chamber, screaming for death. "It must've shattered you to have failed."

"It's not important," you said. "I missed my only opportunity. Now it's in the king's palace at the center of Dromn. Even if I want it there's no hope now. It doesn't even matter."

"There's always hope," I gave you a crooked little grin as my stomach grumbled. "But to pretend to shrug it off like any other lost score. You're a terrible liar. It meant the entire world to you."

You stared me down through the bars with those glorious green eyes of yours.

"If I may offer a dash of wisdom," I said. "Half truths are easier than lies. If you only wanted something a little, don't bother to mention it. If you want it more than the moons themselves, simply say you wanted it enough. Let me know but leave me wondering."

"Okay," you said. "I wanted it enough."

"Very good. And who knows. That may not have been your only opportunity. In another thousand years you might be given a better chance at it."

You rolled onto your back, shaking your head with a long, lingering sigh. "I think not. For all I wanted to use it for, I'm certain a thousand years is too late."

I enquired further but you shrugged me off, explaining again how it didn't matter. You'd had your only chance and failed. The sting of regret wasn't something you wished to discuss.

The first time you truly opened up was when you enquired over my home outside these bars. "I don't feel I ever had one," I told you. "I lived places. I somewhat remember my father's house but I was still young when I burned it to the ground, along with everyone within it. So I've never had any real bonds to keep me somewhere. I spent time in Dromn trying to find a place as a squire in Yossifin's army. That was an utter failure. From there it was Carruga and a while with the Availians at Crystal Bay. I tried my hand at sailing but as a career it didn't fit. There's nothing more confining than a ship in open waters. It brought me to wander the Hyoka Islands for a few years working as a sword for hire. So I can die saying I've seen most of the kingdoms. In retrospect I should've stayed on the northern continent. But there were a few opportunities in Fortia too good to pass up. Paladins to be killed. Treasure vaults to be plundered. So goes the life of a thief. Home is never larger than a half pack of supplies. You go where the work is and all the opportunities are in lands engorged with wealth. Of course you can never settle. In fact, the idea is to have never been seen. When the job is done nobody can question the new man in town or that fellow who splurged for everyone at the inn. But forgive me. I'm rambling. What of your story? Did you have a home prior to our palace?" But you didn't speak. I thought my conversing had bored you into a slumber.

"Mornia?"

"I'm from Hylorn," you said.

My heart gagged on your choler words. The people of Fortia had come to call Hylorn *the Ash Woods*. Rather, *the Ash Woods* was the only name allowed to the people. I myself had made camp there once several years back. On the run and exhausted, one night there was all I'd spent. One night and only because I was too worn out to continue. One night and I'd vowed to never return. But you didn't speak of the land as the nightmare I knew it for. You talked of Hylorn as though it had been some lofty dream.

"My father had built our home for over three hundred years," you said. "It began as a number of saplings, just like the rest of the town. As they grew over the seasons the wood was twisted and manipulated. Some branches were held in shade. Others in light. Wedges and rods were carefully placed in growing seasons to form windows and ceilings. I suppose you saw elfin homes in Crystal Bay though, haven't you?"

"Not like those," I said. I had seen the charred remnants of Hylorn. The tallest trees in the world, petrified into jagged husks. Whatever dark magic Fortia used to scorch the village left it standing ash white and empty. Although it had been years since the town had been killed off for their practice of sacrilegious magic, the was still warm from the fire.

"They're the most perfect homes in the world," you told me. "Living, growing, homes. The rooms were shaped like bubbles up the tree trunks with stairs made mostly of branches. At least half of the shelves and furniture are shaped from the tree, grown over centuries. Moss and lichens were laid to top our beds, although we were fairly modern. Our clothes and sheets were animal hides, except for our traditional priestess robes, of course. My nanima wouldn't have it. They were still woven from the hairs of our people. Everything was alive or reminiscent of life. There was this small brook leading to the Twin Rivers. It passed between three of our trees, with the sitting room resting over it. Every morning when I read I got to listen to the water on the rocks and the salmon fighting their way upstream."

I remembered setting my tent in a dry riverbed. It was the only ground soft enough to stake. But I didn't speak of it. I didn't tell you how I'd seen what became of your Hylorn. I let you discuss your homeland as you remembered it.

"We had bridges of branches, vines, and a little assembly linking all our homes. I would spend days, sometimes weeks without ever touching earth. When it rained we could shower in the treetops. I could pick fruit in one part of the house and harvest nuts in another. We had a small atrium where birds would lay their eggs. My sister used to love torturing them. Blue jays and minkros mostly. They'd all gather themselves in the atrium at night. Kritch would sneak in before dawn and scream or bang a spoon against her cauldron. All the birds would panic but the vines grew too close for them to escape at once. We were all woken up to relentless squawking and panicked chirps. I can't express enough how often I begged father to throttle Kritch for it. And now to hear such chaos again would mean the world."

Of the night and few light hours I'd spent in the Ash Woods the only sounds I'd heard were my own footsteps and breathing. There were no birds, no fish, and certainly no brooks bubbling in the morning. Just silence with an occasional breeze to chill my fingers.

"The whole village practiced in healing magic," you said. "When I was a girl I used to know how to mend mild injuries and cure people of sickness. When there were humans passing through our village I knew a charm to cure them of drunkenness. They never took kindly to it but the law forbade such mistreatment of the self. By the moons they were lucky it was my duty and not my sister's. Kritch was a couple of years younger than I but far more advanced. One time I saw her resurrect a tree frog."

"You can resurrect an entire dwarf," I was quick to add. I glanced over at the few bones and skull that used to be Brugar. Most of his body had been carelessly removed by the guards, but nobody had bothered with the bits of him that broke off when they dragged him out.

"No," you said. "I can sense and manipulate the dead. I can make a body rise if I concentrate enough, but I don't know how to rejoin flesh and soul. I can't return life to the body or restore one's mind. I only know enough to keep a corpse lurking. It's wrong though. You need to understand death before you can embrace life. It's how we learned our spells. The spells to heal wounds are founded on the magic that festers them. The magic of resurrection is founded from necromancy. But we to keep the dark magic controlled. Simple. It's everything our people are sworn not to use once we've learned beyond it."

"How is resurrecting the dead not a dark magic?" I couldn't help but ask. Not in a judging way. Who was I to judge those who could lift the dead? I'd abuse your powers for every depraved act fathomable. But you had my curiosity. It seemed to me that if there was ever a black art, resurrection was it. At least the king seemed to think as much. I'd never pondered the matter enough to disagree.

Still your tone slapped me enough to feel your offense. "It's the difference of giving life to another being or just manipulating a body. Good can come of one but never the other."

"But resurrection is still defying the king's gods," I said as a realization swept over me. "I remember the town criers saying Hylorn had been exterminated by the king for practicing witchcraft. But that's not true at all, is it? Your magic is ancient. It's more powerful than his gods so he was threatened by it." I cut my conspiracy theory short as I noticed the tears carving riverbeds through the dirt on your face.

"They're the same gods," your voice broke. "We worship the same gods. Men wanted cities and the moons drove the shores to build them cities. All we ever asked was to commune. The gods taught us to commune. But men. Men had their cities."

I started to apologize for my speaking out of turn but it was too late. From the sadness in your eyes I couldn't help but think back. When I'd camped in Hylorn, I emerged from my tent in the morning only to realize why the riverbed had been softer ground. It had the faintest brown tint and was littered not just with pebbles and rocks but also broken skulls, ribs, and bones. Broken swords and deformed armor were lining the edges. After the slaughter of your entire village, someone rounded up all the remains and threw them into the river. Probably to wash all their sins away. The moons cleanse the waters. As the river dried out in a barren land all of that decaying flesh turned to soft soil. "You want to raise them, don't you?" I asked. "Your family, friends, and neighbors. With that amulet, your magic may be powerful enough."

You stared off for a long while, scowling at nothing in particular. The same look you give whenever you talk about the killing of men. "The humans took everything," you said. "The souls of my family have been separated from their bodies for so long, even if I had the power to bring them back who knows what state they'd be in? They may return as zombies or worse."

"But you were willing to risk it?" I asked. "To try and steal that amulet?"

After what became a growing bubble of silence you rolled away from me on your little pile of straw. "It matters not," you said to the far wall. "I'm trapped in here. Hopes and dreams are meaningless for the next thousand years. And I tire. Maybe I can sleep some of that time off. Wake up and only have nine hundred years left to my cell. Or better still not wake up at all."

"Mornia," I said. "I'm sorry."

You didn't answer. I didn't know what to say. I remained quiet in my cell. The thought was to let you rest although I doubted you'd so much as closed your eyes.

Minutes became hours. Hours became the night. I felt I'd offended you although I was uncertain as to how. The minutes bludgeoned me and I felt a wound growing in the depths of my throat. It was shortly before feeding time that I finally broke. A growing fear was of the guard sliding the bowl into your cell and you passing my portion over in a difficult silence. Or simply eating it all yourself. Or perhaps even letting it sit until it grew cold and the guards forced it down your throat. All those outcomes weighed over me. You were the first gift of kindness I'd known in far too long and I feared that in my questioning I'd sullied it all. I had to speak to you again, to hear your voice. But I struggled to find the right words. It wasn't as though I could commit to something as casual as, "Oh hello, Mornia!" and hope you were feeling conversational again. More than anything I wanted to find a sentence that would bring you a little hope, a little happiness. It wasn't enough to restore myself in your favor. You were holding me to life and for it I'd insulted you. My words had to be a gesture of gratitude. They had to be perfect.

I hate to admit it but it was the growling of my stomach that let me find them. "How would you like to escape?" I asked, staring up at the darkness over my straw mat.

I didn't look, mostly out of fear, but I heard your joints crick as you rolled on your bed.

"How many dead can you manipulate at once?" I asked.

Yet another dragging moment of dreaded silence, but you finally said, "Maybe five if I concentrate. But it's tiring. I don't know if I can for long."

"If you were stronger?"

You didn't answer.

"I need you to stop feeding me." I said.

"No," you said, a tremble in the words. "No. If you think I'll allow you to die so I can use your corpse for a distraction as I make my escape then you're wrong. I'll not allow you to sacrifice yourself."

I couldn't hide my smirk. You evidently thought me a better man than I was. I was touched. I also became acutely aware that you'd already thought up an escape plan in the event of my death. My feelings on that remain conflicted but I couldn't fault you for being practical. "I thank you, milady," I said. "But I had no intention of dying in a cell while letting another go free. The guards realize that there's an escaped prisoner stumbling about and all of Jerbaisy goes on high alert. What you need is a distraction that will draw their curiosity."

Short of a week had passed when some color returned to your cheeks. You yelled for the guards to collect my body. The first guard who entered our chamber simply beat you and left. A day later and another brute of a man returned to discard me. He knelt over me and sniffed at the air. "Oh he's right gone he is," the guard said. "Straight to the Starless Black, I'd wager. Took him long enough."

I held what little breath I could cling to. I made no motion as he nudged at my shoulder. "Still warmth to him," the guard said. "They says he set yesterday."

"Please just take him," you said. "Please. I can't bear the sight any longer."

"Oy!" the guard punched the bars. "Ain't nobody said you was to talk!" He nudged again at my shoulder. "I seen this game before. If he ain't dead he'll wish he was."

I let him roll me over, exhaling as I faced up. I hadn't accounted for this. I should've. Of course I wasn't the first fool to play dead in prison. The plan was idiotic, desperate. I'd wanted your favor and by thinking with the heart I'd ruined everything before it began. The guard was ready and I was too weak to overpower him. I needed him to lift me before I could strike. I needed him too close to defend himself.

"I known men who slowed their hearts before," the guard said. "I known ones I could pick up and shake about, and they don't make no fuss 'til I throw them in the mokata nest. That's what I does with the corpses, see. Don't throw them in the forest. Don't cast them in the spring. Why you all believe as much escapes me. Whether you playing dead or no, I'm claiming you as food for the dragon birds."

I made no motion.

"Fine with me," the guard said. "Let's try a test, shall we." With two fingers, he gently grazed at my belly. "Come now, Lama. Give us a laugh."

I held myself within. I thought of the trees, the sky, and you spinning freely in a field.

"What are you doing?" you said. "You're twisted."

"Don't mind her, Lama," the guard chuckled. "Think I'll give her a good tickle when I'm done with you." I felt his fingers trace along my thigh. He was backing away. "Think you'd like that? Me tickling away at your little friend?" His fingers moved down the entirety of my leg until he could swipe at the sole of my foot. "Nothing?" He said. "Well if you ain't gonna give us a laugh maybe a scream'll do instead." And then he broke my big toe.

The jolt of pain jerked my leg. I resisted the reaction as best I could but he punished me for pretending. He squeezed down on my foot and then twisted the toe enough for me to cry out. I writhed and the guard chuckled. "Not dead enough," he said, pulling at my leg, dragging me toward him. "Not to worry though, the mokatas prefer their meat fresh."

"Wait!" I screamed. "Wait, no! Forgive me!" If faking death wasn't to work, desperation seemed a worthy tactic. "The king ordered I was to starve!"

"You should've been gone already," the guard said. He grabbed me by the waist and shoulder and lifted, pulling to sling me over his shoulder. "Come along."

Finally. He was over me, his arms wide apart, hoisting me, narrowing the space between us. Weak from starvation and now wounded, I was laughable as a threat.

Perhaps not as helpless as a corpse but only by a sliver. The brute had defeated me once, and was confident he could again. Perhaps that would've been true if they'd bothered to collect all of Brugar's remains after I'd snapped his neck. But it was fitting to the warden, the guards, and likely the king that I should remain with my final victim. I should watch him rot. I should smell the stench of my sins. And that I had. What started as a dwarf soon became a heap of decaying flesh gelatinizing into itself. As the skin and organs rotted to sludge, the bones protruded. I may have been a fool to think I could play possum against a collector of corpses. But how dumb of the guards to think a man couldn't turn his victim into a weapon. They say when a dwarf lacks a pick, his teeth are powerful enough to chew through stone. Strong teeth require deep roots. Small enough to conceal in my palm, a tooth can be a powerful weapon if properly wielded. The pronged roots wouldn't pierce his heart, his brain, or sever any limbs. But the softer layers of his neck offered little resistance as I stabbed him. The guard cringed and I dragged the tooth sideways. Spurts of red gushed in a fountain as I opened the wound. Blinded in blood I heard a gurgle that was likely meant to be a scream. He used the last of his strength effectively, shoving me away, across the cell. A heavy knock to the back of my head told me I hit the bars joining our cells. I dropped to the floor and tried to steady myself, but the pain in my foot overwhelmed and I collapsed.

"Lama!" you screamed. "No!"

I saw stars. I saw specks of light flittering in my eyes. I was weak. Dizzy. I could feel the warmth of my blood soaking my hair.

The guard fell beside me, convulsing against his death. He clutched at the wound, unable contain the life flowing from between his fingers. I watched as he shook and gurgled, his eyes wild with terror. His tears flowed as freely as his blood, and he looked to me, at first with wrath, but then pleading for life. As though some bargain could be reached and I'd undo the damage I'd just caused. But I just watched. My head was heavy and I doubted my usefulness for the remainder of our escape. As the guard's expression calmed and his body gave out, I questioned how long I had before joining him. How long until I was a corpse?

And then he grabbed me.

"Hold still," you said as the guard's eyes began to glow. He placed his hand over the back of my head. He sat up and dragged me toward him, resting me in his lap. With one hand he tore his own shirt and bundled it into a bandage. "I'm so sorry," You said. "It was a foolish plan. I never should've allowed you to try." You began to cry as the dead guard patched my head, your tearful little shivers echoing through him.

"I was the fool," I whispered. The stars were fading along with my surroundings. I'd been saving myself for that first attack. With one guard dead you had a body to control. I was starved, exhausted, and wounded from head to toe. My part in our escape was nearly at an end.

I was unconscious when the next guard, Luthro, saw the door open and stepped into our chamber. What a sight it must've been. With blood everywhere he saw his fellow guard sitting on the floor and my wounded head cradled in his lap. "What is the meaning of this?" His scream jolted me awake. As soon as he was within reach, you sprang at the bars and pulled. I tripped over myself in an effort to assist you. Thankfully my clumsiness resulted in a hit. I fell against his gut, driving him closer to you. Wrapping your arm through the bars you choked him with your elbow. The corpse of the first guard was quick to join, punching Luthro across the face. He became still as soon as the fist met him. Although the corpse continued to throttle his throat, he'd gone limp and you had to brace yourself to support him. Both he and the corpse guard fell to the floor. I, uncertain if you'd strangled him long enough to kill him, dislodged the dwarf tooth from one guard's neck and stabbed it firmly into the other's.

The third guard who entered was Birit and you made quick work of him. As soon as he stepped into my cell, you manipulated the first guard into drawing Luthro's blade and thrust up, just beneath the waist of Birit's armor. He flailed back to the wall, but was felled by the time he hit it. You hadn't even let his body touch the ground before he was your puppet. He stumbled to the edge of your cell and used his keys to open the door. The first guard lifted me over his shoulder and this time I was far more willing to comply. I'd like to have been more involved in our escape, but lacked the strength to stand. I used everything I had to give you the first guard. The rest of our fate I left to you. With Birit's corpse walking ahead of us you used him to pick off additional men. We trailed a small distance behind. Other bodies became other puppets for you to play with. Before long you were manipulating six men, all of which walked in a circle around us. With them you led us through the prison, out the front gate, and back into the world, during all of which, I was but a sack of potatoes. My memories of our escape are few and fuzzy.

I opened my eyes and the first dead guard was holding me over his shoulders. He reeked of death and I wished to gag. I couldn't though. Too tired. Too weak. I gazed at the ground he carried me over. We were in the forest outside Jerbaisy.

You whispered something to me. I can't recall what exactly. I remember your voice was always near, always at the precipice of my being asleep and awake.

I opened my eyes and I saw you sitting on a patch of moss, tending to a small fire. I was resting on a cold belly. "I'm losing touch of you," you said. I couldn't understand what you meant. Was I dying? I tried to hold my gaze on you but it was difficult to focus. I remember your hair in knots and the rings under your eyes. You looked as though you hadn't slept in days. "That's reassuring. Three days ago I had to pump your heart and manipulate your insides to digest. Some parts of you I can no longer control. Your body is doing its own work again."

I opened my eyes and discovered my head was cradled in your knees. Not another dead guard, but yours. You were holding a smooth rock, some bowl like stone to my lips. Your hand was trembling as you said, "Drink this. I already chewed it."

I lifted my head to drink.

I heard the rustle of branches sifting the winds. The warmth of daylight soothed my skin and I smiled. Birds were chatting overhead. Waves -some nearby coast- splashed softly against the shores. I could smell fish cooking over a wooden fire.

Then came the clanks of colliding swords.

I opened my eyes and instinctively reached to my shoulder for a throwing knife but there were none to be had. I surveyed the scene, urging myself to stand, but instead stumbled over and found myself lying in a patch of grass. I was still too weak. Too clumsy.

I stared at the back of my hand. My fingers were thin. I could see my bones. How long had I been withering away? Between the death sentence and however long I was unconscious in our escape, I had no idea. I wriggled my toes and when I didn't feel any shooting pain I realized that my break had healed. I'd been unconscious for weeks. Perhaps a month or longer.

I pushed the thought to the back of my mind. I flexed my fingers to a fist and squeezed. Okay, I thought. Good. I was strong enough to at least grasp onto an attacker. Or better still, one of his weapons. Listening for the direction of swordplay, I wobbled my head around. If I hadn't been spotted in my effort to stand our attackers may have thought I was a corpse. In retrospect, such plans had already failed once, but I'd been unconscious a while then and still wasn't thinking with any amount of clarity.

And then I saw you. But you weren't combating soldiers. Rather I saw two soldiers fighting each other. Their armor consisted of silver chains with red plates. The colors of Fortia. This was emphasized by the falcon claw insignia embossed on their chests. But why were they fighting? And why were you before them, sitting with your legs crossed, leaning back onto your palms?

Beside you was a small campfire with river trout cooking on skewers around it. From their bloated size and royal blue sheen, I'd say we'd been traveling to Western Fortia. Likely a half day's walk from Refecti, a trading post and port most used by whalers. Was that your plan? I wondered. Were you driving us to escape by ship to the Northern continent?

I kept my focus on the soldiers. They swung their swords in wide arcs at one another. Their arms flailed and they dramatically spun about. One soldier raised his weapon over his head and posed for a second while the other brought up his arms to block. The first soldier, instead of aiming for the fingers or kicking while the other's weapon is aloft, brought his sword down, directly against the blade of his combatant. This wasn't a battle at all. I'd sooner have compared it to theater. Theater practice at best. Amateur theater practice. Or perhaps just auditions. For children.

I felt uneasy watching the bout, puzzled not only over the ineptitude of the fighters but their choice in opponent as well. Had the soldiers been attacking you I could see some sense to be made of it. Had they been better fighters, resembling trained Fortan soldiers, I would understand. But these men? Perhaps recruitment in the West has fallen into peril since my arrest. And why not? With the world's most dangerous man locked away in Jerbaisy and all the king's self-declared enemies vanquished, what was left for the soldiers to do but grow fat?

As I watched the battle I noticed how one soldier slouched, drooping his head as though he wasn't even paying attention to the fight. His hair appeared wet and the cloth regions of his armor were soggy. The other maintained an unblinking expression of surprise although I doubted he looked upon anything at all. When he was still enough for me to take in his details I made note of how his nose has been bashed inward and both eyes stared off in separate directions.

I rolled to my side, resting my head in my arms. I tried to speak but had to lick my lips and flex my jaw before I managed to form a few words. "Are those?" I started to ask but failed. On my second attempt I dropped the question and spoke with more certainty, "Those are not the guards you killed in our escape."

You spun around to face me and both soldiers dropped to the ground. The daylight against your black hair shaded your face. I still had no trouble seeing your emerald eyes and perfectly white, elfish grin. "You're awake!" you said. "I knew it would be soon. Last night you began to snore. I think that's how these two found us." As you made mention of the soldiers they both raised an arm from the ground and limply waved in my direction. "And no, these aren't the same men. The guards at Jerbaisy followed us for a time, but on the first night of our escape I met a dryad in the forest. She could tell I was from Hylorn and took pity. She gave us safe passage and promised to throw the guards off our trail. If not for her I imagine we'd be back in our cells. Then all was fine for a while until these men found us the other night."

A dryad? I'd heard tales of tree nymphs and forest spirits but believed them to be tales to spook children. Lessons not to destroy the woodlands or let campfires go unattended. And yet one revealed itself to you. I had to enquire further. "What did she look like?"

"The dryad?" you said with a shrug. "Same as

they all do. Haven't you ever seen one?" To which I shook my head and let you continue. "Chubby, naked elf girl with tree bark in her skin and grapevines for hair. She told me all the unseen worlds feel the empty scar created when Hylorn was murdered. And that she would help us."

"And that was all?"

You nodded. "I hadn't even spoken. The guards were approaching. We had to flee. She commanded the trees and lands to form a labyrinth for our pursuers and then bade me to follow her."

"Oh," I said. I shrugged. What else could I have done? Dryads exist and apparently mourn for your suffering. Thank the abundance of gods for it or we'd be dead. So moving along I pointed to the dead soldiers and asked, "And those men there? You killed them both?"

"Yes and no," you said. "They arrived late a couple of nights ago. I used the darkness to split them apart. There were some dead bats and rodents nearby so I manipulated those into scaring the one away from our camp. Once they were on his body, I could track his movement. Then I used what I think was a bobcat to charge in and bash his face. Once he'd been dispatched I used his body to stab the heart of his companion."

"You had a dead bobcat headbutt a man to death?" I said. My time unconscious, rapping unanswered at death's door, had proven itself as quite the adventure for you. And somehow you carried me along. Come tree spirits and dead bobcats you kept me alive throughout the impossible. "Why not have the beast rip out his throat?"

"I don't know," you said. "I've never bit anyone before. When I was a child I had heard about a dwarf boy who slipped in our river. His family was passing through. I don't remember why. But he fell playing in the river and his face hit the rocks in such a way that his nose concaved into his skull and killed him. I've always wondered if that can really happen. It does." Then after a short pause you told me, "I believe it was a bobcat. It was pretty decayed and I'm unfamiliar with the animals of this region." You then turned away from me, back to the soldiers. After a moment they picked themselves up off the ground and raised their swords in threatening poses. Wavering and clumsy, they began to swing at each other again.

I pushed against the ground in an effort to stand but my legs were too weak. I humbled myself and instead crawled to the nearest tree to prop myself against it. I watched you as you watched the dead soldiers swing their blades. I looked to the campfire and enquired, "When did you catch the fish?"

"Not too long ago," you said. "There's a river nearby, leading to the ocean. I made one of the soldiers lie down in it. As he floated along, the fish approached for a nibble. After enough had gathered, I made him slap them from the water."

I silently laughed a few breaths. "How clever."

"I hope you don't mind," you told me. "I used them to carry you to the river, for a bath. You'd been unconscious since our escape and the odor was... I thought the open air would make you more tolerable, but um. You smelt of the dungeon still."

I look down at myself. The rags I'd grown accustomed to in my cell had been replaced with red trousers and an embroidered purple shirt. "Who did you kill for our attire?" I asked.

"Nobody," you shrugged, watching the dead soldiers loosely interpret combat. "We camped with gypsies a week ago. Strange human folk. And a couple lomin. Maybe you'd have understood them. With no money to offer they were keen on your hair and beard. I assumed that free from prison, you'd enjoy a fresh shave. But do all humans do that? Sell their hair for a place to rest? Should I have held out for something more?"

I rubbed my hand against my naked chin. I'd been growing that beard since my face could first form hair. With a small sigh I felt what little stubble I'd grown in my sleep. "Gypsies are a peculiar folk. Perhaps they produced wigs or required pillow stuffing. In general only the man growing his beard regards it with value."

"I find it's an improvement," you said. And with those words I've never again considered facial hair. "The gypsy women did as well. They were very kind. All of them. And with the elders among their group, we played a drinking game in which the winner gives the loser a piercing."

"Loops," I smiled. "I've had my nostrils pierced shut on account of that wretched game. From the look of your ears, it seems you've won. I hear it takes casks upon casks for elves to lose themselves to drink."

You continued manipulating the dead soldiers into fighting one another. I heard you snicker some but on the matter of the game you said nothing more. I watched you a moment, reflecting on the adventure you had while I'd been asleep. It was such an unfamiliar thing, waking up away from my cell, and yet you managed just fine. Not that I ever had any doubt, but I also didn't expect to be unconscious for so long. Watching you watch the fighters, it didn't take long before I yearned to hear your voice again. "How does it work?" I asked. "Your necromancy."

The soldiers continued to swing at one another. They slowed down some as you answered. "How does breathing work?" you said. "Have you ever seen magnets before? Stones that embrace one another when they're close?"

"Coupling stones," I said. "I played with them as a boy."

"It's not so different from those, I think. It's just, instead of stones, I can feel the dead around me. The soil. The fallen creatures. When I focus I can push and pull them as needed. If their minds aren't rotted away I can sense their feelings. I think. It's faint. I might just be imagining them yell at me as I make them do this." You gesture at the two soldiers swinging at one another. "I've never used a sword before," you said. "If we have any more encounters with the army, I'll need to know how to control the vanquished. To defend myself."

I couldn't help but smile. "Is that what this is?"

"I'm fighting myself," you said. "I'm controlling both soldiers, learning to defend myself against the other."

"You won't learn much that way," I said. "You can manipulate dead men into playing with swords for years and at best you'll only learn to keep up with yourself. Right now your only advantage is that only a few have ever faced a necromancer and the walking dead come as a surprise. Eventually this will fail you. If you wish to survive you must learn proper technique. You must face opponents stronger than yourself."

Both dead soldiers thrust forward and stabbed each other in the hearts. They collapsed against each other, halting themselves from falling.

"You'll teach me to use a sword?"

I nodded. "I used to carve my path as a thief and assassin," I said. "My whole life was combat actually. If not for you all that I know would be gone. You wish to learn to defend yourself? My life is yours to do with as you choose. I'll give you all I've acquired. I'll teach you any weapon you wish."

PART
VI

The palace is empty?

It's not until we've climbed through the window that the eeriness creeps over me. When we battled our way through the streets (or rather whilst you waged war and I was snuggled by a dead ogre) I hadn't taken note of the lack of archers firing from the palace windows. I didn't listen for infantry shouting taunts or lobbing spears. Although I saw brass-belled meurtrières jutting from the palace walls I hadn't found it peculiar that no molten lead or even boiling water rained down from them. I was grateful to be through the fight, glad to have made it this far with minimal injury. I'd been bruised and winded. You'd been shot and your throat nicked. My exhaustion from slaying the orcs weighed at me, but to have made it through Dromn and into the palace meant we'd already achieved the impossible. We'd made it to the heart of the kingdom and all that remained was to twist the dagger. Our victory was at hand. Or at least I thought as much. But now facing endless, empty corridors with the sounds of murder spilling from outside, I feel a void in my throat. The palace closer resembles a crypt than the home of a king.

You whisper, "What are these men defending?" and there is no rational answer. Empty halls and empty rooms? The kingdom's beacon of power and purity is soulless within. Everything beneath its glowing tower of riches is an empty husk. The soldiers aren't protecting their people, nor their government. As far as either of us can see, the war waged outside is over the power of an empty house. Perhaps the men protect only the shining tower and rare treasures? Despite that these are not things orcs care for? Hand them a pile of gold or slice of steak and they'll go for the meat every time. At best the battle outside is for what? To allow Stolzel and the people time to make their escape? This can't be right.

The discordance of war echoes through lifeless rooms. A cacophony of blades clanking, clashing, and slicing overscores the roar and crackle of a city aflame. The grunts, grumbles, and shrieks of orcs duels against the taunts, screams, and cries of men. Outside the palace, the kingdom gags from being eviscerated and fed to itself.

Through the racket we walk in silence. I keep my swords drawn. I take in every corner, adornment, and piece of furniture. I calculate the risk of attack and my strategy against any hidden enemy. These empty halls can't be trusted. We must remain vigilant for anything that might lurk in the dark. I study everything, regarding how I might use it to some advantage. The walls are mostly formed by bricks and mortar. The hard, rough edges may be used to shove opponents against. Scraping their faces along the brick will surely cut them. The flooring is layered by plush, ornate carpet. Its myriad of gold and silver shapes is of little interest, but its cushion softens our steps. Even the tips of your bladed heels are hushed. I like to think of this as an advantage, but any unseen enemy might feel the same. Anyone and everyone in these corridors may use the silence. Although we may be able to minimize our chances of being noticed we still lack the advantage of familiar ground.

Candles adorn the halls opposite each of the windows. None are lit and the only light within the palace comes from the moons and citywide arson. More darkness exists in these halls than light and every shadow makes me suspicious. Through my mask I'm able to see within the darkest cavities. I watch for the slightest movements. The waft of a curtain. The shift of a brick. How many armed men could pack themselves into a hidden passage? How many lie in wait for us to pass one point or another, eager to strike? Should they attempt to surprise us the candleholders protrude from the wall and are sharp by design. They appear to be embedded through a brass cone penetrating deep into the stone. I may be able to break a man's skull against one should the need arise.

We walk slowly. We pass heavy, wooden doors. Their hinges, knockers, and supports are all of iron and brass, embossed to include Fortia's talon insignia. I don't doubt these doors would squeak when opened. Should attackers stand behind any, the initial swing will give us some warning. That too gives me comfort. A silence such as this makes a man feel as though his attacker can approach from everywhere. But no enemy can occupy all space and seem to be nowhere. If someone is lying in wait, stalking us, or preparing to strike, he must reveal himself. Behind a door. Beneath a shadow. No matter his direction, there will be some form of warning.

We reach a bend where this corridor extends into another. A fork in a labyrinth of roads. We do not know the way to the tower and in this emptiness one path is as good as another. I peak around the corner and finally the silence wins me over. "How is there no life in this place?" I whisper. "Perhaps King Stolzel fled the city, leaving his army as a distraction for his escape."

"There's nothing dead either," you say. "I can still feel the fallen soldiers outside but within the palace I only sense smaller vessels. Rodents between the walls. Flies in spider webs."

The silence of the palace is broken. Not through a swinging door, nor an unsheathing blade. Instead we're startled by singing? A lone man's velvet voice blankets over the exterior echoes of battle, draping itself through the entire corridor. His lyrics give me a chill. "*Flies in webs! Flies in webs! Joyous are the spiders when flies shiver in their webs!*"

I put my back to yours and raise my arms for battle. The assault can only come from one direction. In this hall we have both covered. Me with my short swords. You, your staff and rapier. From his singing, I can't determine from where he is listening to us, but he must be close.

I glance to the ceiling. Just to be sure.

The song stops and we're met again by silence. I hold my guard and you do the same. I listen for everything but hear only our breath and the continued battle outside. I wait for another song, a spoken word, the creek of a door, or grind of some stone passage. When no noise comes I grow impatient. The palace is not empty. We have an adversary nearby listening in on our words. Although I'd never admit it aloud, he no doubt has the upper hand. He hears us and therefore must know our position. Given the enormity of the building, to know where we are, he must've known the moment we entered. So it's probable he saw us climb in after the massacre outside. Despite our display of violence, he mocks us through song. So he's not afraid. He's powerful or at least thinks as much of himself. And already I know he's patient. This isn't his first fight. No, he introduced himself through song. This is a game he's played before. Maybe even his favorite game. *Flies in webs*. He wants to see his flies shaking, trembling in his trap. If we want him to attack we'll have to coax his next move. Let him know he's in control. So I give him a reason to keep singing. I show him impatience. "Show yourself, coward!" I scream. I spin my blades in tight loops fast enough for him to hear the spider silk cutting through the air. "Come out and face us!"

It's not enough. We wait. From one silent end of the corridor to the other, nothing happens. I continue fishing. I yell for him, "No worthy foe would hide and sneak in shadows!" To this remark, you give me a glance and raise an eyebrow. You don't even have to say it. My hypocrisy isn't lost on me. For I am an assassin. I'm a thief and a burglar. Even this night began with sneaking along the shadows of rooftops. So I shrug. An opponent worthy of us would most certainly be on par lurking in the darkness and taunting me with song. But why inform him of this?

Another moment of our adversary's silence is enough to convince me that standing in corridors achieves nothing. He will wait. We must explore deeper, perhaps even allowing ourselves to spring whatever trap that awaits us. I look to the nearest room and lower myself to the ground. With my mask I see the legs of a desk, chairs, and the bases of bookshelves. I see darkness and nothing of any importance. No man awaits us in there.

We slink along. At several other doors I peek through cracks and keyholes, discovering nothing remarkable. Beds and dressers mostly. Vanity mirrors and armoires. We've discovered the bedchambers of royal families. At least from times when there had been royal families. King Stolzel, a holy man, or rather a man who regards himself as holy, was brought to power by the deaths of the Yossifin and his kin. Perhaps these rooms are now used for guests. Perhaps these rooms have remained vacant for the past decade, all the death beds still neatly made since the bodies of the old king's family had been removed. My mind begins to wander at the possibility of an assortment of royal jewelry in these chambers. The tiaras and necklaces of princesses. The brooches and bejeweled sabers of growing princes and future kings. What becomes of such trinkets when there's no one left to wear them? And who do I know that would pay half their wealth just to possess them? Not that I'm in any position to loot the entire palace. Not until we've acquired your amulet at least. Certainly not until after we've silenced our singing adversary.

The hall takes us to an alcove of sorts. Potted planters line the walls, draping their vines around plush sofas. Several candles are lit and leisurely flickering. At the center is a statue of the messiah, Xavious, with his arms slightly raised as though preparing to embrace an old friend. Water flows from within his stone sleeves, down his cupped hands and then pours into a ring fountain. Words are written in some language I do not know. But you tell me their meaning. "Gods protect our steward," you whisper, rounding the statue. "Until the return of He." You then turn and look to the back of an alcove. You point your staff toward an ornamented double door. It seems heavy, carved of some glimmering stone and bejeweled with all the colors of the gods. The candlelight gives it all a soothing glaze. "The king's bedchamber, perhaps?" you say.

I step toward it and lower myself. Through the keyhole I see the largest four-post bed the world has ever known. At its side a lute rests on a stand. I find that somewhat amusing. Where I'd keep a sword the king keeps his music. How safe he must feel in his palace. But I go on, inspecting the legs of other furniture. I see gilded tables and mirrors twice the height of man. Lowering myself further, I stare beneath the door crack to give myself a wider view. As I look to the side of the room, I see legs.

I roll back. I stand. Did anybody inside notice my approach? Is our singing adversary within? To you I gesture four fingers, meaning four people, meaning twice as many of them as there are us. Perhaps even the king himself is among them. Which would make the other three his royal guard. Far better soldiers than the infantry outside. Perhaps even worthy opponents. Quietly, beneath the babbling of the fountain, I sheath one of my short swords and replace it with several throwing knives. To you I gesture to pull at the left door. Should it not be locked, should it open, I'll make the first attack.

You nod and go to the door. I take a moment to look back down the hall from where we came. Just to make certain we weren't being followed or have soldiers readying to surround us. With everything clear, I nod and begin my charge. As you pull I lunge myself through the opening. I leap into the air, rolling my body. Should they fire arrows, I'll be a difficult target. Should their aim be precise, my spin will aid slightly in deflecting the attack. And with such an elaborate entrance they won't notice how my spin adds speed to my throw. They won't be ready for my knives flying straight at their heads.

Three knives make contact. The fourth misses. None of the men fall.

I land on my feet and rush the one I missed. I bring my sword down hard into his shoulder but stop myself before the blade makes contact. My attack will

114

have no effect on him. He is a statue.

You dash into the room, your staff raised and ready to strike. But in an instant you see the battle is over with my ego lies defeated.

"My hero," you jest.

I pluck my knife from the first statue, a burly dwarf with his arms crossed and a stern expression on his face. The blade takes several chips out of his chest.

"What is that?" you ask as I move to the next statue.

It doesn't fully occur to me to look at the entire display of statues until you begin to approach them. The first is the dwarf, followed by a man with his arms up, slightly crouched. It's as though he were about to fall to his knees. Perhaps protecting himself? His head is turned to the side as if to hide his pained expression. Next to him is a tall, stoic elf, his hands clasped together in prayer. The last is another man, bearded. He stands with his head down, his arms at his sides. Ashamed perhaps? Disappointed?

My throwing knife pierced the ear of the second statue. I pluck it free as I gaze on this most unsettling art. "These are not meant to be gods," I say. "Nor are they valiant. Each of these men appears defeated." As I say the words, staring at their ash white texture, it creeps into me that I've seen something similar. In trees.

"Perhaps they represent the tribal groups," you say. "Stolzel had the dwarves near Bermisk killed along with the wood elves. Then there were the plainsmen who didn't recognize him as king. The other man I'm not sure about. Perhaps another tribe. There were several other groups who resisted his rise to power."

I ponder the art, rolling my throwing knife between my fingers. If memory serves, there were eight villages exterminated in Stolzel's initial rise to power. Hylorn was the first. The others shortly followed. Anybody who resisted the king or didn't come to love him were erased from the world. If these statues- A warm wetness on my fingers stops the thought short. I stop rolling my knife and look down, spotting blood all over my fingers. But- I hadn't felt the cut. There was no pain. At least none apart from the usual soreness and aches of battle. In my confusion I look to you and your eyes are fixed on the second statue. I look to the ear, where my knife had pierced. A stream of red is leaking down its neck.

"The statues are bleeding," you say. You step toward the crouching man, tap his ear, and immediately pull away. "It's soft," you say. "It's flesh."

No. No, that can't be. So I run my finger along the ear, and sure enough it feels no different than my own. Continuing, I move to the statues face, and its hard as rock. I rap at it with my knuckles and it knocks no different than stone.

I rub my fingers on the elf statue's ear, discovering it is equally soft. I look to where I freed my blade from the dwarf. A pool of blood coagulates in the wound.

"My gods," you say. "By the moons. These are people. They weren't carved. They were trapped this way."

From the halls, the voice returns. "*You found the old regents,*" he says. I can't help but feel that our adversary is smiling.

We raise our weapons to the door.

The voice continues, "*At least they each could have been. Had they proven their worth to Xavious and the Gods. Now they just listen and carry the secrets of a man they should've lived up to being. Their penance for not leading their people on a righteous path is to be their own living tombs.*"

At the mention of the name *Xavious* I throw my knife straight into the back of the fountain in the hall. It plunges deep into the statue. The thought forms that our adversary had been posing as messiah's statue. When no blood trickles down into the water I decide against the theory.

"*Oh now. One of you is becoming frustrated,*" the

voice says with a mocking froth to his tone. *"Be gentle with the regents. They are eternal now, but do still feel pain."*

It begins to occur to me that our adversary only spoke after we had described something of our location. He listened to our conversation but must not be able to see where we are. He interpreted the sound of my knife stabbing the Xavious fountain as my attacking one his statues.

You lean to me and whisper, "I think he means to coax us out of the bed chamber. Why would he otherwise choose now to speak?"

I nod. Perhaps I can play that against him or draw him toward us. He mocks these stone men. He belittles them. They are of no true value. His savior however is likely of greater importance. So I tell him what happened. "I thought perhaps you were posing as the fountain. So I threw a knife into its back."

I'm right. A cough echoes through the halls. It sounds as though he's clearing his throat. An attack on his messiah is incomprehensible. I'm sure it's some kind of violation or sin. While the blow may not have been a direct punch, I'm certain my effort hit him where it hurt. And he's quick to scold me for it. "You desecrated the champion of our lords?"

I answer with another knife, straight into the back of its head. Then another into its backside.

"You," he says. His voice darkens. "You insufferable, black blooded orc child. Do you realize my gods punish every race? Do you not have any shame beneath your clammy skin?"

"He does not," you say.

I turn to you and again you shrug. And again I cannot argue. If I felt the tactic would be effective in breaking our enemy, I'd proudly urinate into that fountain's water. But it seems unnecessary. From how he speaks to us the man thinks we're a pair of orcs who made it through the ranks of the city. He most definitely cannot see us, nor does he suspect us to be more intelligent creatures. The fact that he speaks to us in the Fortian native tongue tells me he knows quite little about orcs at all.

"Then he'd best be taught a lesson," our adversary says. "He must witness the strength of the gods first hand."

You lean toward me and whisper beneath his continuing rant. "He doesn't see us. I don't know how, but I don't believe he's near. Somehow he only knows the sounds we make."

I agree. Our opponent is in the castle but maybe not as close as we'd believed. I don't doubt this palace holds more threats than his voice but at least from this man we are presently safe. So I begin to leave the royal bedroom. You do the same, but stop suddenly, waving a hand for me to look. You gesture back into the halls. Just beyond the alcove, you point toward one of the candles. At first I don't see its significance. It had been there when we arrived. It remains at the same angle. From all I can tell, the flame isn't poising an arrow at my heart. But as the man's voice continues to speak, I notice how the light of the flame seems to vibrate in unison with our enemy's words.

"For the great moons see all," he preaches on. The flame shivers to his sermon. "They cast light in the darkness. They cast truth in even the blackest of hearts. And for this, we sing. We celebrate in their power."

Although he continues, I pay little attention to his words. I instead approach the candle and inspect it closer. The entire base trembles with his words. I begin to notice how it isn't fixed to the wall, but rather funnels into it. The candle sits just outside the bell of a horn.

That's how he hears us. I point at the little bell, and you nod. You even gesture to the other flames in the alcove and indicate how they're all vibrating with the words of our enemy. He can hear us through the candleholders. "And now, vile orc children, we will sing a hymn in praise of our lords."

I look to you and am met with rolling eyes. Clearly the man's voice is beginning to vex you. But what are we to do? Cover every candled horn in these halls? No, no. Just let the man sing as though his words hold meaning.

And sing he does. *"There is the light of the gods! Tis the fire of immortals! Praise be to those in darkness! For their way is lit!"*

He repeats the song, and at the word *fire*, every flame in the alcove extinguishes. In the same instant you wince and bring your hand to your ear. I look back and forth for some attacker but there is none. Just us, standing in darkness. Throughout the halls, the only light is that of the burning city outside.

Our adversary continues his song and you drop to your knees. *"Praise be to those in darkness! For their way is lit!"* he sings again. And then flatly he says, "Come to the light, my darlings."

"What is that screeching?" you whimper, rubbing the mask over your ears. "Is he setting canaries aflame?"

I get close to you, looking for a wound or mark. "His singing?" I ask.

"Beneath it," you say as you recompose yourself, adjusting your mask and giving your staff a quick spin. "Or with it. I don't know. You didn't hear it? That piercing?"

I shake my head and the sound of a lute begins echoing down the hall. It's a slow melody, soft with fluid, calming notes. And to it you wince. I look through the halls for an attacker, but it doesn't take much to determine the music itself is what's hurting you. The tempo increases and you double over. It begins to ascend in a scale, and you cover your ears, shrieking back at the high notes. And then as music peaks into an almost unnatural octave, two things happen. You fold into a ball on the ground. And in the same instant all of the candles in the corridor ignite with rich, ruby flames.

Their heat is intense and for a moment I can't help

but shield my face with my arm. But I return to you, kneeling down and proving myself to be a useless mess. I can't stop the music coming from each of the candleholders, nor do I know how to shield you from it. You're already covering your ears so I place my hands over yours. For all the good it does you. Even with the both of us muffling the sound, you continue to squeeze into yourself and cry.

"Come to the light, my darlings! Come to the love of thy lords!"

You scream out over the music, and I join in hopes that we can drown out whatever it is about the song that's hurting you. I try to find encouraging words, to raise you to your feet. "Collect yourself, Mornia!" I scream. "We have to keep moving. We have to escape this." But it's as though you can't even hear me. I doubt you even notice my hands over yours.

"Come to the love of thy lords! Come to the light, my darlings!"

From behind I can feel the heat of the candles roast my back. I glance over my shoulder and see the flames have grown to the size of men. Those further down the hall are even larger, expanding far enough to meet one another, and then they begin rolling toward us.

"That noise!" you scream out. "Stop that noise!"

"The noise!" I realize. Your mask doesn't merely amplify light like mine, but sound as well. Whatever hidden sound he's plucking beneath his music, your mask allows you to hear it. I grab hold to tear it away but your hands are pressing so tight that it won't budge. And whatever fabric it's made of seems impervious to my pull.

The flame continues to grow as it reaches toward us. Even worse, it's picking up speed. There's no time for your mask so instead I sling you into my arms and run for it.

We don't make it far. You're writhing and screaming, "Make it stop! Make it stop!" Carrying you is like being ridden by a bucking bronco and before long I trip over my own foot and stumble forward. I drop you. My chin meets the floor. My teeth ensnare my tongue and erupt a geyser of tears. I watch you land feet first, twist your ankle too far, and collapse back into a ball.

I see sparkles dance in my eyes and am no doubt bleeding from the tongue. But can't let it slow me. As the flames sear my feet, my only option is to move forward. I pick you up and sling you over my shoulder. "Ha!" I say, accidentally spitting blood onto the outside of your thigh. "Light as a feather, milady! Like running with a twig!"

"Come to the light, my darlings! Come to the love of the lords!"

My making light of things doesn't help and the flames are coming faster. I push myself harder, noticing how the candles liquefy beneath their erupting fires as I pass. When I see ruby fires growing at the far end of the corridor, I round a corner and start down another hall. All the while you're kicking and flailing. Your knees keep jabbing into my gut while your elbows repeatedly grind into my back. I'm fairly certain you fracture one of my ribs, but won't let it slow me. The heat pushes us forward.

"Come to the love of thy lords! Come to the light, my darlings!"

I skid around another corner and trip over my own foot. We crash into the wall, but I manage to keep from falling. At the far end of the corridor I see the flames coming toward us. Behind us I feel the fire nipping blisters into my heels and elbows. I continue running, breathing in metal flavored air. Ahead I see a golden glow from one of the rooms ahead. Still fire, but natural flame. Not this burning magic. So I push myself. I charge straight for the room. With the red flames encroaching from ahead and behind, I do my best to increase my speed. For the effort I cough. I feel my lungs ready to spasm into a fit. But I hold it in. I keep going forward. The heat of the flames burns at both sides and just before they can engulf us I pivot into the room, leaping forward, and throwing you ahead of me.

The song comes to a bravado finish and we slide across a marble floor. I gasp. I choke on my own cough. You're lying face down, twitching and clutching your mask, not even reacting to the few spots where your hair is ablaze. I stumble halfway into a stance, but collapse forward. "Mornia," I hack out and roll onto your hair. You scream out as I smother the flames. I'll apologize if we make it out of this alive. "Be still," I tell you, but you don't seem to notice. With the fires smoldered I rip the mask from your face and tear the remaining fabric from your ears. You jolt at my touch, cupping your hands over mine as you cry on the floor. Your arms from your shoulders to your gloves are cherry red. Your face matches except for where the mask had shielded you. Blisters and black charring are everywhere.

You whisper a single word. "What?" And after a few hard coughs you try again and ask, "What was that?"

I roll off of you and onto my back. I take deep breaths, trying to calm my heart. I make fists and curl my toes, taking a quick inventory of myself. I crick my neck and click my jaw a couple of times. My tongue is bleeding. I feel warm everywhere.

The voice of our host slithers ominously around us. "You are not orcs," he says. "Why have you come here? Did you think you could hide while your comrades defended our city? Did you actually think such sins would go unpunished?"

You look at me, tears in your eyes and blood in your ears. I think your expression means to play along, to act as soldiers, but instead you say, "We should ask you the same thing. Where are you hiding? Dromn is half dead. Maybe the city would've lasted the night if someone of your strength had joined in the battle."

The voice tells us, "The kingdom needs its palace. A palace needs its king."

"Stolzel," you say, gritting your teeth.

I roll and lift myself onto my knees. After a few long breaths I bring myself to stand. My breaths are heavy and I can taste the stink of myself. All this running on rooftops, fighting in a war, and outrunning magical flames has exhausted me. But I can't slow myself. Not now. Not when we've made it this far. I reach down for your hand, stumble, and hoist you onto your feet. You lean against me, and when I look down I see you're keeping one foot elevated. A faint whimper in your voice is all I need to hear. Whether or not we find this amulet, I'm not leaving the palace without the king dead.

His voice rises as he says, "You are not my subjects. Why have you come here? What are you doing in my home?" I can't help but notice how clean his voice sounds. There's no echo like back in the corridor.

I stretch in a few directions and let myself hurt. The night is far from over and I have a feeling that pretty soon I'll have to put the pain aside. If our host, the mighty King Stolzel, doesn't decide to let us go and get back to our thievery, then he'll strike up another song and start smacking us against the walls. So I take in the aches and pains and prep myself for more. I start looking around, automatically seeking escape routes and hiding places. Of which there are none. We're in an enormous hall. Multiple red banners hang in layers over each of the walls, all of them embroidered with man-sized emblem of a falcon's foot. I want to ask you if it's the same symbol that forms the amulet we're seeking, but I don't because I'm uncertain if Stolzel can hear us whisper. So I continue looking around.

There are no windows. The far side of the room features an altar with an ornate, wooden and brass chair at its center. And even as I stare at it, it takes a long moment to realize that we're standing in the throne room. The belly of the beast, so to speak.

While I take in the sights you begin to form a lie. "We're travelers," you say.

I look up at the ceiling and see that red banners are evenly stretched over the entirety of it. Smaller banners hang down to accent those on the walls and ceiling. And at the center of it all is an enormous, brass chandelier supporting dozens of candles. The entire structure is made of enormous brass bells. They're just like the ones behind the candles in the corridors but larger and formed into a sort of brass bouquet.

"Vagabonds?" Stolzel's laughter fills the hall. "You claim to be some sort of gypsies? No, no. I heard sneaking, swords sheathing, and your boy destroyed the statues in my bedchamber. You are no mere travelers. Your intentions are malicious."

I can't help but repeat, "*Boy*?"

"Very well," you nod. And after a deep breath you look up to the horn bells above us and say, "My name is Mornia D'Onnyxa. My companion is Lama Percuor."

"Your name proceeds you, Miss D'Onnyxa," the king says. "To think, what days of ruin I am living to see. My entire kingdom struggles against the orc invasion and now even the unholiest of creatures stands in my very throne room. An elf. A putrid necromancer of an elf."

I can't help but bring myself into the conversation, "And Lama Percuor. The legendary assassin and king amongst thieves. Tis I!"

A sharp note from a stringed instrument causes all of the banners in the room to flap and I'm thrown immediately to the ground. The king screams, "You are nothing!"

I look to see where you landed, and notice the sound had no effect on you. You're standing, supporting most of your weight on one foot and your staff. So it seems he can focus his music in this room. Lucky me.

Strings begin to play again. It's not his lute any more. It has a deeper, richer sound to it. A cello, I think. But he isn't yet playing a song. He's tuning the instrument. Over the notes he begins to laugh. "Lama Percuor," he says. "*The Fish Thief of Luna Falls*. One of my advisors, a fellow named Godfrey Hecklebrook, drafted the order for your death. It seemed you murdered his cousin. A farmer by the name of Jasper. Tell me, as a man of so many sins, do you even remember him?"

I remember Hecklebrook Farm. I'd attempted to hide with the slave workers while running from the local authority. Normally a flash of steel is all it takes for slaves to cooperate and offer a space on their floor. Hecklebrook's workers had asked that I pay a toll. The stomach of their master for a night's rest. It had seemed a fair trade. But I say none of this to Stolzel. Instead I give him the man he knows me as. "Reveal yourself, good King. Let's discover how long I'll remember your name after claiming your head."

He chuckles, tuning his instrument. "To think I used to pray for you. The only man I ever sentenced to die. I prayed to the gods even as I signed the order. 'Help this foolish man find your love. Give him peace and the opportunity to restore his soul to your favor.' I said those things for you. The very worst of all mankind and I begged for your immortal soul's salvation. And it seems my prayers went unanswered. For here you are, in my own palace, the dog of a witch and just as savage a killer as you ever were. Perhaps the gods are still teaching me what it means to be king. Surely they wanted me to see that not all men are deserving of my righteous words."

You've had enough of his lecture. To the brass bouquet you yell, "The only man you sentenced to die? The only man? And what of the elves of Hylorn? The dwarves of Rising Rock? The wandering people of Suncrose, Abrigall, and the Tornado Plains? Did you pray for their souls? Did you pray for all those tribes and villages you had your army execute? Did you seek the gods' favor when you had your countrymen slain in droves?"

Stolzel plays a sharp note and you turn your head as though you've been slapped. The blister on your cheek starts leaking blood. "People?" Stolzel says. "Mornia, you foolish witch. The moons gave man the world. Its creatures are for us to use to become plentiful. I've thanked the gods many times for my meals and the gifts of animals who labor for the benefit of man. But I don't pray for soulless beasts."

"Monster," you say. "We all pray to the same gods."

"A trick that I think should teach such beasts to know their role. But I suppose it must be difficult for simpletons to understand. And to call the wandering tribes people reveals how savage the elf-kind are. Those who do not seek the true path of the gods, or those who lie with creatures like you are blemishes on this holy kingdom. Through the purification I have brought the true people to light. Perhaps if the wandering people and wood elves had played their part they wouldn't have found themselves as holy sacrifices. They could live like the mountain elves in sanctuary, praying for my holy guidance. But no. They fell into black arts. Godlessness. Praying to spiral winds. Healing wounds meant to scar. The animals of the wilds grew too distant to be tamed. They had to be put to rest before their infection spread." He plays a short scale on his cello, followed by several more sharp notes. With each one, I see ripples travel along your dress. "Why have you come here, necromancer? All this way with a war at your back. Did you truly come to chastise your King for tilling the soil of his lands? And dirty my castle by bringing your dog in tow?"

"My king?" you say. "I came for the *Magneouxecrex*. But I think I'd rather leave with your head."

He chuckles and plays another couple of notes. "You think yourself worthy to claim my amulet? I can only imagine what darkness you would devise with it. Very well. Very, very well indeed. I was saving my strength in case the orcs made it this far but perhaps a little warm up is in order." He then begins to play a song. We both brace ourselves to be thrown in the air or pushed to the ground. But nothing happens. As I look around the throne room I notice all the banners are beginning to flap. The king says, "Very well, necromancer. Very, very well.

With one so in tune with the dead as you, I think you'll find this melody particularly pleasing. I call it *The Bone Dancers*."

He strikes several quick notes and all the banners begin to thrash around with the music. Dust is lifted from them and the floor trembles with every note. Specks of dirt and pebbles all rattle along the marble. And then I feel something brush against me.

I turn. There's nothing. More magic. I look to the torches, expecting more flames to meet us, but the fires lighting this room don't react to Stolzel's song. The smoke however seems to be wafting in our direction.

Another chord begins and something nudges at my shoulder. "Do you feel that?" I ask.

The notes increase in tempo and I watch as you spin around, swinging your staff out at nothing. At first, I find it an odd time for what looks like a kata, but as your staff spins, it strikes- something? Nothing at all actually, but I hear the thunk of wood and your staff shakes from the impact. A bit of smoke wafts at the space around you and for a second I think I see a skull hanging in the air. All the little particles on the ground are shaking toward it. As you swing and strike against something else, I see the smoke and dust begin to form the shape of skeletal feet on the floor.

And then I'm struck with the urge to duck. There's no attacker. There's nothing to cause the sensation but I trust my instinct to go through with the motion. Enough fights and battles have taught us both to trust our senses. And for that I'm grateful. As I twist out of the way of an invisible strike, a tear slices through the hood of my cloak. There's no time to question it. I draw my blades and swing out at where I think my attacker stands. Although I see nothing, I feel my blade connect. My weapon and entire arm vibrate at the strike. It's as though I've swung to hit a wall of solid rock.

Out of the corner of my eye I see you're spinning your staff, ducking, and twisting around against some unseen attacker.

I look back to the space I'm pushing against and as a higher note plays, for a just a moment all the dust in the air locks in space, taking the shape of a broadsword. A break in the song causes it all to fall and crumble away. But as the music begins to pick up, all the little particles catch in the air. Parts of the blade are reformed. Arms, legs, and ribs take shape.

Another several notes and when I look to you I see skeletal hands and feet. Helmed skulls are swinging axes around you. You twist and dodge as they appear. When you block an attack it shaves a sliver from your staff.

I look back to my attacker and watch as it forms. Up close, I can see the little flecks of dust and dirt floating through the air and then suddenly being captured. They vibrate against nothing and then are joined by other flecks. Little by little, the specks take the shape of a ribcage, and then plates of armor. The dirt on the floor becomes boney feet. As the tempo of the song increases, the full figure of an armored skeleton begins swinging wildly at me.

I roll back. I block several attacks. Each one shakes my entire arm. When I block a heavy swing the trembling is so powerful that I nearly drop my sword.

I catch glimpses of you fighting, mostly dodging attacks. You flip backwards onto the throne, and then jump behind it as an axe comes down and stabs into its seat. Little splinters of wood fly up along with bits of fabric and stuffing. They quickly circle in the air and ripple into the mass of your skeleton attackers.

"Can't you control them?" I scream over the music.

"They're not skeletons! They're not of death!" You yell back, rolling onto a knee and knocking an attack to the side. You twirl your staff and hit one of your attackers square in the face. Bits of particles scatter everywhere, and the skeleton even stumbles back a little. But more importantly, the king's song screeches an off note.

Continuing to defend ourselves, our eyes meet for

just an instant. A brief, knowing moment. Despite his tricks and powers, this enemy is no stronger than any other. Striking these opponents hinders the King's cello. We found a weakness. We can defeat him.

But for all the encouragement that comes with such a thought, it quickly dissipates as the song continues beneath the king's laughter. "Ho-ho! Was that you, necromancer? Or was it your pet? Let's up the tempo, shall we?"

He starts playing faster and fiercer than before. The skeleton creatures also begin moving more quickly in turn. Their bodies become denser. We both dodge and duck around their swings. Those we block cause our arms to tremble. I manage to land a few swings and stabs of my own and each one is met with an off note. But my opponent is too fast for me to hit anywhere critical. Maybe if I wasn't already injured multiple times over I would be more successful. But with the wounds already present and knowing that this fight is only beginning, I have to conserve myself. Giving everything now could result in having nothing left later.

You're less cautious. When I catch glances of you, I see you twirling your staff and landing hits like you're fresh in the fight. Although you keep your weight off one foot, it doesn't stop you from kicking with it. As for your staff, I watch as you throw it like a spear at the head of one opponent. It rebounds off of him, back toward you. But instead of catching it, you duck beneath, letting it pass over you and hit the other attacker in the chest. Little particles plume from their bodies. Some even land in the space of our attackers and are reabsorbed back into them.

The notes are off key but the song continues. It grows faster and louder.

You deflect a hit from one skeleton while kicking off the other. Between them, you roll under one swinging axe and then jump over the other. You near the wall and both skeletons lunge at you. I think you're about to stumble, but instead you grab onto one of the banners and hoist yourself over your attackers. You then kick off one of their helmets and grab the banner even higher.

I block several more strikes from my opponent and notice your staff spinning through the air toward me. I sidestep, which my opponent anticipates, causing him to turn. The skull of your staff hits directly into the back of his neck, or the space that makes up the neck area of him. I'm not really sure. But he stumbles forward and then dissipates into a cloud of debris.

A string on the king's cello snaps. Stolzel screams, "What have you done?"

I catch your staff and am about to throw it back, but you're not even fighting any more. Both of your skeleton attackers are swinging their axes up at you but you're far out of reach, climbing the banners up toward the ceiling.

I want to call out a number of things. "How did you do that?" "What are you doing?" But anything I say will be heard by the king. And if I had to guess, glancing at the brass bouquet of pipes above us, you already have something in mind. So while both of your attackers are still trying to reach you, I seize the opportunity and throw both of my short swords at them.

Two clouds of dust explode.

Two cello strings break at once.

"How's that for a nothing?" I yawp and pound my chest.

"Well, well," the Stolzel's voice sounds through the room. "First A. Then D and G in the same instant. I was focusing on your better, but was it you who broke all three of my strings?"

"Start playing the fourth and we'll find out!" I yell. I watch you as you reach the top of the wall and grab a fistful of the ceiling banner. You swing off the wall and start making your way hand over hand to the middle of the room.

"Ha!" Stolzel says. He actually speaks his laughter. "And what of the necromancer? Was she helpless without her powers? Have I struck her down already?"

I can't help but grin. "Milady has more talents than you can imagine," I tell him. "To think you can kill her with a little song and dance is quite amusing though. Horrific as your music is, she can certainly stand against it."

As you near the brass bouquet, you point for your staff.

"Let the lady speak for herself, whelp!" the king commands. "But very well. If you think you're ready for a challenge, I suppose the orcs aren't coming any closer. I was preparing a new symphony for them but perhaps I'll try it on you instead."

You hold out your hand and I throw your staff up to you. Then to the king I say, "Let's hear it."

"Very well," he says. "I call this *The Wave Dragon*."

A high screech of a note chills the air. All of the banners on the walls begin to wave and ripple. But just as soon as the song begins, you swing your staff and smack the largest bell on the chandelier.

"Ah!" the king screams. Your attack pained him. "What was that?"

I laugh. Up above, hanging by one hand with your staff in the other, I watch as you grin. You swing your staff and smack the bell again.

"Stop that!" the king screams. He starts to play, and all the banners begin moving. Some of them shake so hard that they rip. On the floor, all the dust and dirt that made up the skeleton soldiers begins to shake and lift into the air.

You smack the bells again. Everything drops.

"Oh, you're quite amused by this aren't you?" Stolzel says. "You think you've defeated me? Very well. Allow me to open a few more chambers." He then grunts and all of the banners shake. Another grunt and they all ripple and fall.

More urgently, you fall with them.

I scream. I charge forward, keeping a steady eye on you as you drop. As you near the ground, I feel my heart skip a beat at the thought that I won't make it in time. So I leap. I jump forward as hard as I can and reach out. I'm not nearly as graceful and strong as the dead ogre you'd controlled, but I still manage to break your fall. We roll and slide forward as several banners fall over us.

"Are you okay?" I ask as I catch my breath and fight for an opening around the banner.

"I doubt it," you say.

"You still want this thing?" I ask.

"I suppose," you say. "Why? Do you think we'll encounter any danger getting to it?"

I grin. I can't help it. I grin and tell you, "That's all I need to know." And then I manage to work my way out from under the banners. When I look over, you're starting to stand as well. We smirk at each other but the satisfaction of surviving another moment is fleeting. With the banners all fallen and carpeting the floor, we see that the entire throne room is lined with enormous brass bells. Each one is the size of the chandelier and directed at the floor.

"Now then," Stolzel's voice comes through hundreds of pipes as he plays the same sharp note on his violin. "*The wave dragon.*"

PART
VII

It took close to a year for me to give you this night. I'd been forming the plan for quite some time prior, or at least asking myself how it could be done. How do we, two of the most wanted criminals in Fortia, get ourselves all the way into the heart of Dromn? How do we break into the palace? How can we sneak our way up to the highest tower, and steal the amulet, and then get all the way back out with our lives?

I've always been a fan of misdirection. The trick is getting an entire city, the army, the palace guards, and the king himself to all look one way while we stroll in through the other. Let them know something is afoot, but keep them focused on the wrong threat. I never could've predicted an empty palace or that the king had such powerful magic at his command. But until tonight, as far as plans go, I thought it went rather well. Better than expected.

My first idea had been for us to infiltrate posing as soldiers or diplomats. People who would have access to the palace, or could at least obtain it. But that throws in an entire mess of variables that are wild and unpredictable. How well do the soldiers know each other? How are those closest to the palace chosen? Once inside, what are the routes to the highest tower? How many people can one expect to pass along the way? Are there any enchantments or spells we'll have to diffuse? Traps to avoid? How do we even get to where we're going? And how will people react at the first sight of your long, pointed wood elf ears?

One doesn't simply acquire the layout of the most heavily fortified building in the entire world. And if caught behaving suspiciously in any regard we would most definitely have an entire kingdom at our heels.

The risk was never worth the reward. For seven years, we stayed as far from Fortia as we could. After we fled Jerbaisy we spent some time alone in the forest with you nursing me back to health. Exhausted and malnourished, don't think I've ever forgotten how you watched over me. You hunted for me. You fed me. Once free, you could've left me there to starve, but you continued to sustain my life, just like you always had. It was a kindness I'd never known.

Once back to health, it was my turn to aid you. At the time I believed I could offer you a new life. I thought that if you could begin anew then perhaps over time the wounds of your past would callous over. But they would never heal. How could they? It wasn't merely a parent, a friend, or a home taken from you. It was your entire life; your entire world. Everything you'd ever loved, petrified into rock or burned to ash. I knew of no remedy for such agony. But I thought –I hoped– I could give you a life to move on to.

Of course I was a mere murderer and a thief. A lowly human at that. The only life I could offer was the one I knew. So we began stealing together. We began sparring. I trained you to fight. I pushed you to wield your necromancy, testing your limits and forcing you to exceed them. From there we began to see the world. Not Fortia proper of course. But we traveled to all the other lands in the many kingdoms. Within two years, our reputations preceded us and we began taking work for those who would request our skill. The dwarves needed us to steal metals from the elves. The elves needed us to sabotage a human encampment. The humans required a Fortan diplomat assassinated, as they were certain he was to blame the recent struggles with the dwarves and elves. We drifted along, one journey to the next. From one heist to another we were always a step ahead of the world.

For my part this was living a dream. Always on the move. Always uncertain of where we'll be in a week's time. One adventure after another with the beautiful elfin warrior who held my heart. But it was never enough for you, was it? I'd see the light in your eyes in moments of danger. You loved the heat of battle as much as I. You felt alive as we'd sneak our way into dragon dens or rob the riches off of traveling aristocrats. I remember a particular con you came up with, the one where you'd offer your services as a priestess and raise a recently deceased long enough to settle any debts or inheritances. Who ever gained the most always paid for your puppet shows. Usually ahead of time. Oh, how you'd laugh at all the foolish human faces as you made the dead loved ones flail around.

It was at night that I'd always see the other side of you. Something you were struggling to hide. In those quiet moments when we were alone and could be ourselves, that's when the pain of darkness was revealed. You'd drift off, silently staring at the moons or our campfire. You'd cry in your sleep and grow miserable at a moment's notice. Whenever I'd ask what was the matter you avoided the issue or only say a few short words over that amulet or your people. A random rant at the evils of mankind here. A wish for their death there. And what was I to say? I was there to stop your bleeding if a job went wrong. Or place a splint around a broken bone. These injuries that ingrained so deep in your heart I lacked the expertise to mend. How does one fix the blind hatred of an entire nation? What manner of damp cloth could I place on you to soften the sickness of being a lone survivor?

For the most part, your actions and incidents of wrath were expected. I thought little of them, or at least knew they were natural. But there was that night in Hyoka. We'd made camp on the side of a mountain and were drifting to sleep, gazing at the stars. A thought had been lingering in the back of my mind for years so I finally worked up the nerve to ask. "Mornia?" I said. Although you didn't respond I continued with my question. "They say there were no survivors from the Ash Woods. I mean–Hylorn. None. I've always wondered, and you needn't answer if you wish not to. But I've always wondered how it was that you survived."

After a long silence you told me your gravest secret. You said, "I didn't."

I looked to you in awe but was met with only a

shrug. It reminded me of our discussions in Jerbaisy all over again. Except that I was seeing you within another type of cell. One of your own creation perhaps. Yours and Stolzel's.

After several long breaths you told me the tale. "When I woke up I was naked, looking up at an altar, draped over a shattered resurrection rock." Then after another long silence, you told me, "There had been a pile of bones at the foot of the altar, burned and petrified like everything else. When I looked closer I saw they were heaped over a small staff. My sister's staff. I don't recall dying. Just the flames all over my village. White and violet flames. Then there was an arrow piercing my face. I fell and that was it. A second later I awoke in the church. Kritch must've survived the initial attack and carried me to the altar. She must have performed the life ceremony as our village was being destroyed. It's the only explanation. She had never attempted a resurrection on a person before and neither of us knew the ritual. But she was powerful for a girl her age. It's the only answer I can come up with. She cast a spell and died so that I might live."

"I don't understand," I said.

"When she set me on the resurrection rock she had made a choice. She could've tried to flee but instead she tried to save me. Even with the spell cast it takes time for the soul to rejoin the body. I don't know how long I was dead. One minute Hylorn was alive. The next it was that husk they left behind. I was groggy for days but remember a pair of footprints in the dust. Faint, barely there. I don't know why but I assumed they must've belonged to a Fortan man. Probably the last one to step foot in my home after he'd destroyed it. I swore I'd kill him. With all my heart I swore against those footprints. It was the only direction I had so I took it. Not that it got me anywhere. I'd been wandering for eight months or so before I heard Hagglesburge had been sacked. I remembered the wizard, so I went to see if I could claim his prized possession. And you know the rest."

Your heart became clear in that moment. "With the amulet," I started to ask, but felt hesitant. I never told you this but it was a selfish thought that held me. I wondered, with the powers of your magic enhanced, would you leave me behind? All the other questions were there. Would you be able to bring your people to life? Not just raise their bodies but also restore their souls? And despite my earnest love for you I wondered what use you might have for me if you could return to the life you once knew. I'm a mere human. Not even a good one. I ached at the thought but didn't allow myself to utter the words.

You answered the question you thought I was about to ask. "The most powerful spells I know couldn't resurrect a blade of grass in Hylorn. With the amulet, who's to say?" And then you rolled away from me.

I watched you sleep that night. For a time at least. You were fitful. Sad as ever. I'm slow in some ways, and for all our time together it took that conversation to finally understand. For whatever sort of life I might offer, I could never be your home. None of my doings would bring you peace. I gave you myself and everything I knew. But this wasn't what you needed. There was no hope on the path I offered. No home or promise of a future. Just more death. More scraping by on dirty deeds until we'd buried ourselves too deep in them. For an elf you were still young and had an eternity ahead of you. I had aged several years since we'd met and didn't know how long I could truly survive. Especially with how I lived. What would be left for you after I'd grown too old for this game? Or if I'd even live to see being too old for this game? I am ashamed to admit this but that night I'd thought to leave you behind.

The thought didn't last. Clearly. It was actually a dream that brought everything into focus. I saw the two of us, beaten and tattered, standing at the edge of the Ash Woods. You turned to face me, speaking, but not in any language I knew. In your hand was a falcon's claw. You held out to me but when I reached for it you recoiled.

Then you bit into it. Or rather devoured it. You gnashed the claw in your teeth with blood spilling from your mouth and spraying on the white earth beneath us. Once the claw was gone and your hunger sated, you turned back to the petrified trees and solid ground. You stepped forward and as your bare foot hit the ground, plants began to sprout. Another step and dead shrubs blossomed with life. Hummingbirds flew from the tears in your clothes. Snakes and squirrels alike sprouted from the soil and fanned out into the petrified forest. Every place this new life spread became green, brown, and alive. The river filled and flowed. Even the pale sun became more vibrant and gold. With every step you took, the Ash Woods grew and returned to the glory of Hylorn. And as you reached one of the great tree homes, you were greeted by your kin. Elves. Two of them older, a man and a woman. And a girl, perhaps a teen. They all greeted you with open arms and smiles dampened by joyous tears. It was my wish to be a part of it, but as I reached for you, to join you, to be a part of everything right in your world, I saw that my hand was bone.

I awoke just then, and the sun had risen. You were sitting in the grass, whispering to a spider as it crawled around your fingers. It was the first time in my life I'd felt heartache and loss but I embraced it. Fortia had stolen everything from you and celebrated the massacre of your people. I couldn't have helped matters, offering the life of a rogue, teaching you to embrace your darkness and use necromancy for such gains. You deserved better than this, milady. You deserved happiness, peace, and love. There was no guarantee the amulet could amplify your magic and restore anything that had been taken from you. But if there was any chance for a future it was in that trinket. I swore then to myself, if this life with me couldn't bring you the joy you deserved, I would give you the only thing that could.

It took time.

It took planning.

How does one break into the palace at the center of Dromn, climb to the highest tower, and escape the city unnoticed? How do you get every single inhabitant to look the other way when you're a known criminal in those lands?

The way I saw it we'd need an army to get into Dromn. But brilliant assassins for hire that we were, there was no nation that would volunteer for such a campaign. Instead I had to improvise.

Three weeks ago I sat in a pub at the center of Bersmick. It was a mining town at the edge of the Fortan kingdom, bordering the wilds. Or more specifically, bordering orc territory.

It had been a quiet night, and I sat alone, sipping a bitter wine, listening to vague attempts at music coming from a warped lute at the far end of the pub. Just another traveling minstrel, I thought as a way of distracting myself. Truth be told, I mostly thought of you. It had been nearly a year since I'd set my plan into motion. And the greatest sacrifice of it was to leave our life behind entirely. I became Grubas, a hand for hire in the mines, unearthing gold and gems so they might be polished, melted down, and assigned values or enchantments.

It was all part of the plan. If I was successful I'd be seeing you shortly for the first time in ages. But I had matters to put in motion before I fled town.

I believe the pub was called The Magic Gem or something else equally clever. I'd snuffed out the candle at my table, as was my custom. Whenever the barmaids asked, I said staying in darkness helps me see better in the caves. In truth, I found the bit of shadow made it all the easier to observe my fellow bar patrons unnoticed. And they were, like of all Fortia, a horrific and revolting crowd. Or at least one convinced of its destiny to sit above all else.

The men carried on their tradition of berating the elfin barmaids while singing and celebrating over what was simply another night of drinks.

"You there!" a miner said to his waitress, a young elf woman with bruises on her arms and a lack of sleep in her eyes. When she failed to hear him he stepped on the chain she dragged between her feet. The poor girl nearly tripped on her shackles, but caught herself. She was used to the surprise. "You there!" the miner said again with a laugh. "Another round for me and my mates."

"Of course." She bowed as she'd been trained.

"And quit looking so glum," the miner said. "Give us a smile with your service."

The poor girl curled her lips, revealing a half set of shattered teeth. To which several of the miners laughed. They sent the girl away unharmed this time. But this was far from their first encounter and the night was still young. Of course no one would argue this treatment of the child. According to them, according to their king, the elfish folk were meant to be punished for their sins against the gods. Where Hylorn was burned away from sin, the other tribes practicing their own relations with the gods were in fact defiling the moons. They had to learn to live in servitude of greatness again. So the elf nations who were loyalists became slaves. And it was the people's duty to use them as needed. For the sins of one race may be used as the reward of another. King Stolzel had poisoned all his people, warping them with a sickness that made them always right and always unaccountable. Funny how the cruelest and most twisted of people are always those chosen to stand over all others. My year in Fortia allowed me to see it in this town and in others. The kingdom's people were righteous. Along with such piety came the obliviousness of evil.

"Grubas!" several of the other miners greeted me and sat at my table, uninvited I might ad. "Grubas! Always sitting alone! Always with that serious scowl." The one who boasted my false identity was the pit boss, a

Lomin named Arpsmith. As he and several other miners sat around, he continued, "I tell you boys, I swear Grubas would be toiling over woman troubles if he'd ever make time for one. Always in the caverns. Always hard at work."

"Someone must be," I whispered with my usual sneer. Grubas was not a happy disguise. After joining the village, he found the local authority, Fortan soldiers, to be corrupt and uncaring for the safety of the working civilians. It was their duty to protect the workers from the local orc threat. And as there had been fewer and fewer orcs in recent years, the soldiers had become bored. And fat. Like all men of authority who lose their necessity, they began turn against the workers as a way of securing their position. They began with tighter restrictions on gem inspection, making sure none of the miners stole by having them turn out their pockets. Then they began searching homes during the day while the miners were at work. And of course, some of them began to exploit the situation by stealing from the mines and the homes of workers themselves.

This was entirely my doing. Between shifts, I was slaying the local orcs to give the guards less to do. Pretending to be concerned with theft, I'd suggested they add security posts in the mines to discourage such behavior. I then planted gems in my most respectable coworkers. Little by little I appealed to the greed of the soldiers while making conditions worse on the community. And as life became increasingly hostile between the two groups, I kidnapped several miners and murdered them in orc territory. Not deep within. Just far enough to grab the attention of the local orcs. Enough for them to send scouts and spy creatures to keep an eye on the town. Then when I returned and people were speaking of how villagers had gone missing, I began telling the miners how such a thing never would've happened if the soldiers had been protecting the people instead of policing them.

Now, all around, the people were talking under their breath. And Grubas was just another scared and angered gem miner, worried over the next orc invasion. And that's as much as I told Arpsmith. "How many more of us have to disappear before the soldiers see what's happening here? Why weren't they in the shafts? Why do they stand at their little checkpoints and offices while we're underground? What if we dig into orc territory? Who will defend us? I cannot fight. Can you?"

"I can swing a pick," Arpsmith said. "Regardless of what it strikes it always does the same job."

"I admire your confidence, friend," I said. "But orcs raise swords. Orcs sling arrows. How are we to fight them when it is clear nobody cares to see them coming?"

"And what do you propose?" Arpsmith smiled. He was a fat little beast, smaller than a dwarf with a burly, feline face. An oddity in this part of the world, his grin was easily mistaken for a scowl. I knew the difference, but few others did as well.

"We take this to the soldiers," I said. "We demand they deepen their search for the lost. We demand they lead at every tunnel. We force them to quit their corrupt ways and give us the protection and respect we deserve. And if they won't, we'll write the king himself to send us men who will."

"I doubt you'll find much favor in such conversations." Arpsmith shrugged. "Our guards don't care enough to risk their hides in orc lands. And I doubt King Stolzel can afford to send us replacements. Not with all those zombie outbreaks on the far side of the kingdom. Moon minded men of valor are months away from our lot."

It took some time and several more drinks but eventually I was able to bring Arpsmith and some other miners around to my point my view. As the night rolled on I became louder. The miners' anger grew along with mine. And when there wasn't another drink to be had or a mining song to be sung, I bade a large group of men to not return home and rape their slaves but rather put the energy to use and show the soldiers what we thought of their actions.

It worked. Arpsmith himself toted his position and played some drunken politics so that it was he who led the charge to the command post. With everything in place I was able to sneak off and take my own route to the guard's station. I was even able to dress myself in a Fortan soldier's armor, complete with a quiver and bow. By the time Arpsmith and his comrades were at the gate, loud, drunk and disorderly, I was at the peak of the guard's tower with an arrow already notched.

"Go back to your homes," one of the soldiers commanded. Several others lined alongside him, swords and clubs at the ready. But his order was barely heard by the crowd already yelling insults and profanity. "Calm down, everybody!"

Arpsmith stood at the head of the rabble and squared himself against the soldier. "Why don't you go home?" he asked, tapping his finger over the soldier's armored heart. "For all the good you do us. Send us soldiers loyal to the kingdom and not their own pockets."

Words were exchanged and tempers arose on both sides. For the soldiers it was a matter of dealing with drunken fools. For the people it was for the dismissive tone of the soldiers. Not that it mattered what either side said. I'd spent nearly a year dividing this town and making the kingdom turn on itself. Nobody would listen. Nobody would back down to opponents they couldn't respect. Teach the people that everything they do is right and you'll have rotted their compassion or the willingness to see others' side. These were the teachings of King Stolzel hard at work. And now all it took to crumble the kingdom would be a single arrow. An arrow I pointed straight for Arpsmith.

"For you, milady," I whispered to myself as the soldiers and miners continued to argue. "For the kingdom that wishes us dead, poisoned by its own grandeur. For what these people did to your home, I swear they'll never be given opportunity to do to another."

I loosed my arrow and Arpsmith vanished from view in a spray of blood. All became silent until I screamed out from the soldier's side, "They're firing on us! They're firing on us!" And so all the soldiers joined in the attack. And as the drunken miners heard my voice in that same call, along with the random dead comrade, they all began striking as well. Arpsmith was right. Regardless of what a pickaxe strikes it always does the same job.

I started several fires on my way out of town along with some other acts of civil unrest. Just to heighten the drama. Just to further alert the orcs that Bersmick's defenses were down.

Much later into the night, I went for a stroll down a quiet road. It took several hours, and it wasn't until I was worn, exhausted, and knew I couldn't possibly go any further that I finally heard your voice.

"Were you successful?" you asked.

"I believe Dromn awaits us," I said, nodding to the shadows. You rode out of the darkness on a carriage led by a single horse, lighting a small lantern as you approached. Oh, Mornia, to see your green eyes again after a year was more soothing and whole than a sunrise.

"Lama," you said, hopping down from the carriage. "You're bleeding. Everywhere."

Having been in the dark all this time, I truthfully hadn't noticed. But as I looked down at myself, I spotted a number of wounds and gashes on my body. "I'm not certain it's all my blood. I had to fight my way out of the town," I said.

"You were supposed to escape before the fighting got out of hand."

"I know," I said. "But things escalated quickly. There were a few matters I had to handle before I could flee on good conscience."

"Well come inside," you told me. "Tell me everything and I'll tend to your wounds."

You lead me inside the carriage, which I noted as having engravings of a distinctly holy nature. Along with the finest woods, it seemed constructed of ivory, silver, and other rich materials. This must've belonged of some wizard or priest. "You've been busy," I said as you sat me on the floor and began stripping me of my blood soaked clothes. I gestured around us to the carriage.

"There were some mountain elves who weren't as loyal to the kingdom as they claimed. They supplied me with the carriage, disguises, and some weaponry. They sharpened all your blades too."

Oh, my swords and my knives. How I missed the many tools of my trade. I daydreamed a moment over finally holding a short sword again as you unpacked a bag of assorted bottles and cloths. Your healer's kit. Tools of another trade, or rather from the life you should've had if not for Stolzel and myself. Slowly you lifted a shimmering blue bottle, and then poured some of its contents onto my shoulders. Circling around me, you knelt at my back and began wiping my body with a sponge. "What happened to you?" you asked.

I took several deep breaths. I let myself feel your caring hands tend to my wounded flesh. "I was nearly out of town," I said, but hesitated. I caught myself confused by my own actions as I reflected over them. "But I went back." Your hands stopped. I continued to speak. "There were these slaves. Elves and human heretics. Some ogres and dwarves. Mostly younglings. Not children, but young. I couldn't leave them all to die. Not over my actions. Those who celebrated Hylorn's demise are being given back the pain they caused. But those who were trapped there didn't deserve it. At night most of them were housed in the same two barracks. And the basement of a pub. So I went back and helped lead as many as I could to safety. Some soldiers fought me. One of the ogres panicked and I had to put him down before he killed the others. Stupid creature. Anyway, I didn't save everyone. Just whom I could. I would've gone back again but the orcs were beginning their advance. I had to get those I saved away from the chaos."

You rubbed a lotion along my muscles began smoothing it across my arms. Your touch was gentle and warming. "Lama Percour," you said. "It seems there's a good man in you after all."

I blushed. I don't even mind saying it. I blushed. I watched as you stuck a small variety of leaves in your mouth, chewed them into a paste, and then applied it with your lips over my gashes. "Still a rogue, milady," I said, trying to remain calm from the softness of your lips. "Our enemy is Fortia and they weren't a part of our fight."

Tying off bandages over my wounds you said, "I'm glad of it. But what happened to the people you saved? They're not following us, are they?"

"I gave them direction by the stars and sent them toward the hills," I said. Turning my head, I felt loose. The medicine from the paste was beginning to have an effect. "If they avoid the open road and stay off the orcs' scent, they'll reach Ara before long. I suppose I left them to chance. But some chance is better than none."

You nudged me into lying on my back and poured oil over the bruises on my chest. You then sliced a mushroom and lined its parts along my forehead. "This will extract any poisons or disease that may have entered you through battle," you said, pressing down on the mushroom and smearing it over my skin. "It will also make you rest."

"Nonsense, milady," I said, although the effect of the ointments and medicine was already taking hold. I began to feel warm. Perhaps even drunk. "I want nothing less than sleep. I just got you back. The past several months I've heard tales of zombies throughout Fortia. I always wanted to be there. To see you make them," I said, looking into your eyes. You said nothing back but instead smiled and continued to mend my wounds. I raised my hand to touch your face, but only made it as far as your thigh. "This is what you should've been," I said. "A healer. You've always saved me. You made me better." I may have babbled on some more but my eyes grew heavy. The medicine was taking over. I felt your hands cleaning a gash across my gut. "You're beautiful," I said, smiling, drifting off to sleep.

I awoke the next day in a hood and a loincloth.

PART
VIII

Outside the palace, Dromn screams with the sounds of battle. The clash of steel swords. The thunk of wooden shields. The crackle and roar of uncontrolled fires and boom of boulders launched from catapults add to the insanity. Men and orcs alike all call out into the night. Some are yelling out their victorious boasts. Most are screeching at their deaths.

Inside the palace a violin plays a gentle melody. Its song is soft with a sad, sweeping charm. Every note lingers like teardrops on the edge of my chin. Under other circumstances I'd probably even think Stolzel's song resonates with me.

"Go!" I scream. "Go! Go!"

"Get up!" you yell. "I'm not leaving you behind!"

Outside the palace, every street is soaked with blood. The orcs and soldiers fight on rubble, stumbling over the ever-growing piles of their fallen comrades. Flames blaze over the carnage burning away the war and charring those who still fight it.

I would welcome the chaos of the streets any day over this song.

"Use the travel stone!" you beg over the music. "Save yourself!"

"Not a chance!" I yell back.

All we can do is run. Through another corridor. Down another hall. The floor shakes and the walls tremble. We go up a flight of stairs and the music follows. The music awaits us in every room. We dash through a dining hall and the tables vibrate into the air and shatter to pieces. The splinters and boards all become a part of it. Everything does. Shards of glass. Loose tiles from the floor. Painted canvases and their frames. The fabric of the palace banners. Displays of armor and weapons. The beast moves through walls. Pieces of the walls break free to become a part of it. The fires from the very torches and candles lighting the palace are caught within its invisible body. But once within even the flames are squeezed. They ignite the other broken things. They spread and smolder, highlighting the shapes of organs in a creature that doesn't exist. The fires show a heart beating ash. They show lungs purging dust. They show pupils widen and lips curl as the creature thunders toward us.

"Don't look back!" you scream over the music.

But I can't help myself. I have to see it. I have to face it. For all the times we've faced death and thrown ourselves into danger, nothing has ever been so invincible and unimaginable as this creature manifested from four strings and a bow. I have to look my death in its eyes of glowing embers. They're the only part of the beast that stays constant and I can't tell if they're really watching me or just a shape formed from the music. Does the song bring it to life or is it Stolzel's own empty puppet? Its claws scrape the floor and its tail dents the walls. How can it just be a song? What unworldly magic makes this from a song?

We reach the end of the dining hall and are about to enter another corridor when I glance back again. You scream to keep moving but I throw a knife at the chandelier hanging over the beast's head. The rope breaks. Brass bells and iron rings fall. The beast jerks its head at the impact and shivers as the metal snaps, fragments, and bends to form a jagged spine. The beast sneers at me, flaring its nostrils and filling its lungs.

The king had called it a wave dragon.

It doesn't roar like an animal, let alone a dragon. It doesn't breathe fire and it doesn't belittle us in the ancient languages of its kind. It just draws back and then unleashes an unworldly, thumping blast. The floor ahead of it shatters in waves. And if I hadn't looked back, it likely would've ripped us apart. It's done this attack several times already. It threw us into walls and around corners. It bounced me off the ceiling and scraped half the skin off my arm and your shoulder. But this time I'm ready. Having already faced this roar four times I brace myself and leap toward you, grabbing you and pulling you close.

The wave throws us forward. We fly down an entire corridor, spiraling through the air. Even when my feet land against the far wall, the force is enough to keep us from dropping to the ground. It's a futile effort but I look at the dragon and scream back at it. No specific words or even an attempt at language. Just one violent roar against another.

The thumping fades and we drop to the floor, hitting it in a run. You're limping but I still push my hand against the small of your back to keep you moving. Or to keep myself moving. I have to get you to the amulet. After all we've done, even with death at our heels, I will not fail you. We will see this night through.

"Keep up!" you yell over the king's music.

The wave dragon's claws appear through a crumbling wall and slash along the corridor at our heads. We both drop, pressing ourselves against the floor. I feel the entire palace tremble as its talons pass over me. Although it misses my face my hood gets caught and drags me back until the fabric rips. I stumble and continue running forward, just behind you. We're nearly into another room when the dragon's wing comes down through the ceiling and smacks us both to the floor. The vibration shreds my clothes and rips my skin. As the wing rises, you're being hoisted. Your hair is caught in its wing, or forming part of its wing, or whatever it is that happens when things get too close, and it's raising you toward the ceiling. I stumble to my feet and jump onto your back, knocking you back down. Your head jerks as locks of your hair are plucked free. You yelp. As the wing passes back up into the ceiling, I see several long, black strands float back to the ground.

We double back. The claws and wing were headed

in one direction so we head another. The damage to the palace is catastrophic. The carpet is in ribbons. The walls are missing entire sections of brick. Even the brass pipes being used to manifest the dragon are protruding, twisted and dented. It's the sight of those that keep me from speaking. If the king can hear us the dragon can spot us. So we limp along silence, nudging into each other's shoulders and fighting our bodies to breathe slow and steady.

After who knows how many paces, you begin to slow down. Defeat is in your eyes. The night has vanquished you and I know it'll be impossible for us to escape the city alive. If the dragon doesn't get us the remaining men or monsters will. But this can't be the end. Not limping along in a hall when we're this close. So instead of an agreeing nod of defeat, I wink. I can't hide the pain, the bruises, or the fact that I'm bleeding from several places I'd forgotten I even have. But to you I still give a wink and a smile. To you I try and convey, "It's just another adventure, milady! Just another Black that we're passing through. We'll be through it soon."

The wall ahead of us explodes. A boulder tears its way into the palace. You stumble back and I fall. As if the wave dragon wasn't enough, now the orcs are within catapult range. I lie on the ground, weak enough that I don't want to stand. But you're still on your feet and for that I must continue. You offer your hand and try to pull me up. When you can't we use the wall to support us both. Little by little we gather ourselves. We look to the outside through the palace's new opening. With all the running and fleeing from the wave dragon, I hadn't realized we were already several stories higher. From here we can see all of Dromn. What isn't red from blood is glowing from flames. Everywhere, the battle rages on. From the streets to the rooftops, the Fortan army continues to stand against an endless force of orcs. And in the midst of all the disaster we see the catapults being wheeled ever closer. And then another volley of boulders launches into the fiery night sky.

We duck behind the wall for all the good it'll do us. Thankfully none of the boulders collide nearby. I can still feel the floor shake from the impact.

We look back out over the chaos and death; over the absolute ruin we've caused. Above the fires and madness I look to you and smile. Perhaps I'm overwhelmed slightly in the moment. All these fires and the carnage of battle, I can't help but reflect on how it all began with a single arrow. A small riot became a full on orc invasion. I shot the arrow that brought down an entire kingdom. This was my gift to give you a chance at peace. So I listen to the screams and blazing battle of Dromn. And then, most unexpectedly, I feel your knuckles graze along the back of my hand. When I glance down, I see your fingers coiling around mine. I squeeze my fingers between yours and let myself feel warm.

Outside the palace, a chunk of building fired from a catapult smashes its way through the side of a tower, causing an entire building to tilt and crash down on a group of men and orcs alike. Within minutes soldiers from both armies are atop the rubble, continuing the fight, their weight undoubtedly crushing any surviving comrades below.

Inside the palace we're watching the world end hand in hand. Somewhere in the back of my mind the feeling can be conveyed in the simple thoughts of "oh," and "finally." But the battle isn't over. You start looking out the hole in the wall, off in the other direction. "The tower," you whisper. "If we stick to this corridor, the tower is just ahead."

Then something trips us. Something knocks us down and drags us outside. I reach back and grab hold of a brass pipe. Our fingers slip and you're being pulled into the night sky, rising and stumbling to stand on a floating piece of floor. As it flies out of the palace, dust and free particles collect. The ashes of the city give the wave dragon a darker, somehow even more sinister appearance.

And you're on a piece of flooring that's grinding down into the creature's body. "Mornia!" I scream.

You leap out of the sky and back into the palace. The boards you were standing on disintegrate, taking on a new form as a scaly back with spikes protruding from a spine made of music. The wave dragon flies from the palace and straight into another volley of boulders. It roars and the nearest rocks shatter. They become part of its body. The further ones are only deflected, falling down into the mayhem of the streets below.

Safe for a moment, I turn back to my present circumstances. I'm hanging by one hand from a brass pipe with a little bell at the end. That same song is ringing through. I try to lift myself but my fingers slip against the brass. I scream out your name again and through the pipe, over the bastard's violin song, I hear the voice of the king. "You're still alive?" He then sings some random note, causing the entire pipe to shake. I curse as I fall. I reach for the palace in hopes of some traction but merely scrape my fingers. I pass the window of the story below and your hand reaches out and grabs my wrist. I smack against the wall. When I look up you're holding onto me, hanging halfway out the window.

"You went down a flight of stairs?" I ask.

"No. The dragon ripped out most of the floor," you say. "I fell right through." And then after a prolonged moment of my staring into your eyes you tell me, "This really hurts."

I take the hint. I dig my other hand into the palace wall and do my best to find footholds. It takes a moment of scrambling, but before long we're both lying on our backs, breathing and collecting ourselves. When I look around, the walls and ceiling are in ruins. More importantly, the nearby pipes are dented and twisted shut. So for the moment we're safe. For the moment it's okay for me to look over and ask, "Are you sure you want this thing?"

You roll your eyes. "I don't know," you sigh. "The

night is still so young. Maybe just that dance and some wine. We'll see where the evening goes from there."

It takes a few minutes to help each other to our feet. We use what's left of my cloak to bandage our wounds. Some shreds of the palace make for adequate splints. I'm tempted to ask if you feel me dying but am nervous over the answer and decide against it. I pat myself down, hoping to feel a throwing knife or dagger anywhere on me. Sadly my entire arsenal is long gone. We have nothing left, but stumble down the hall, straight for the tower. We both look out the windows as we pass them. The wave dragon continues to defend the palace and roars waves of destruction down onto the streets. Little orcs and Fortan men are being thrown around in the distance.

We arrive at the tower and ascend its endless spiral of stairs. The violin music continues to blare, and I start to get a feeling that I know exactly where the king has been hiding. I mime the motions of the violin and then point up the tower. You nod. All the pain and exhaustion leave your face. In your eyes I see only anger.

You climb the tower faster than me. If anything I'm slowing you down, practically crawling as I ascend. But you keep me going. You're moving forward and I have to at least see your victory. I have to make it until the end.

High, high above the city, we finally reach a doorway to the treasure room. And to my absolute amazement it's open. Not even just ajar, but wide open. You walk freely into the room lined with stacks of gold, jewels, and the entire wealth of the kingdom. There's no wave dragon, bone dancer, or even common soldier waiting to ambush us. Just piles and piles of luxury. I slide myself in and smile. We actually made it. And sure as the night is black, at the far end of the room King Stolzel stands on a balcony made of brass pipes and little belled ends. He dances to the sound of his own violin in an awkward series of convulsions while dragging his feet and swaying his head. He isn't even aware that we're behind him. I'm tempted to rush him and shove him off, but first there's the matter of what we've come for. Where is that stupid amulet?

You limp straight for one of the pedestals. On it sits a rather ordinary looking item. A dark stone with no luster. It's carved in the shape of a claw and if I had to guess, it's probably that of a falcon. When you grab it, you immediately hold it up to me and smile. I nod and watch your eyes as you marvel at the little trinket. A stone that enhances magic power. Something that in the hands of a healer can mend injuries in seconds or even wipe away fatal diseases. But in the hands of a necromancer, who knows?

As you stare at the falcon's claw a look of puzzlement creeps over your face. You squeeze your fist over the stone and sneer. "Your highness!" you scream over his music.

Stolzel jumps, startled, and spins around to face us. It's not at all a shock to see that he's a withered, older man than the portrait from back in the church. His hair is gray. His chin sags like the dark robes he's wearing. His eyes have a cold intensity completely unlike the portrait. About the only thing identical to the painting is that he wears the same black crown. He's added to it though. Assorted gems are lined between falcon claws, all of which are just like the one you're holding. Watching you, he doesn't quit playing his song. How can he? He's commanding the wave dragon to protect the palace. Should he stop playing the orc invasion will be that much closer to victory. "You!" he says. "You must be the necromancer." And then to me he says, "You, I assumed would be thinner. Not much of a boy at all though."

"The stone," you say, holding up the amulet.

His face grows red but his eyes stay cold. He regards you for a long moment as he plays and then turns back to his burning city. "Fine! Very well. You have what you came for. Take it! You've won. Now leave me to defend what's left of my kingdom!" There is something priceless about the moment. Here we are, two thieves in the king's own treasure trove, standing with the very man we aim to steal from. With all of his power and how easily he can defeat us, instead he's forced to defend his palace before the catapults can bring the whole thing down.

"I think not," you say. "I see your game. Most bards are weak with magic. They can manipulate others with music. I've seen one manifest something as large and as fierce as a kitten. But skeleton warriors? An entire dragon? This truly is a rare sight."

"And I should've killed you when you first stepped foot in my home. My decision to play with you is one I'll live to regret for ages, I assure you. But the battle is over. Look at yourselves. You can scarcely stand let alone fight. You're in no position to do battle with me and unfortunately I'm too occupied to crush you. If I stop playing we all die. So I say we call this a draw. Take your little souvenir and run. If you're lucky my men won't find you."

You laugh. "This isn't a draw," you say. You goad him. "You're playing your sad little song over our victory. You see, Lama started a riot in Bersmick. All it took was a squabble between the villagers and local infantry to draw out the orcs. He did that. And none in your kingdom could've prepared for what followed."

Stolzel misses a note. Somewhere along the palace wall, a boulder strikes. He recovers from the blow almost immediately and continues playing. He looks out over all of Dromn. I like to think he's letting it all sink in. All the orcs and his fallen subjects were the result of the two people he just tried to dismiss. He continues to play and says, "You brought this upon me?" In the distance, the wave dragon swoops down and roars. Hundreds of orcs go flying. Some of their bodies collide into the dragon and are ripped to pieces, becoming a part of the thing that killed them.

"Tell me it hurts," you say. Your feet drag as you approach the king. Blood runs from under your bandages and spots the floor beneath you.

Stolzel slowly turns around. He continues to play his song as he stares us down. "You. Imps of the Black. You murdered my kingdom." Off in the distance, the wave dragon turns in the sky. It circles around until it's facing the palace.

You laugh. You stumble a bit, lean against one of the pedestals, and laugh. You hold up the falcon claw. "This amulet. This is a fake. I feel no different. All the riches in the world are here but you put a fake in your tower." The claw drops from your hand and lands with a few drops of blood. "You know its power. Sad, weak, little bard."

The king continues his song. Far, far behind him the wave dragon flaps its wings and roars at the streets. There are screams. There are buildings falling into rubble. Stolzel screams at us as his dragon approaches. "Murderers! Monsters! You killed everyone! You murdered my entire country!" Spit flies from his mouth as he screams. His dragon is coming closer.

You take another step forward, still supporting yourself on the pedestal. "We finished the slaughter you started. All the sinners had to die. Every last one of them. You killed me. You took my family. You burned Hylorn down to nothing." Another step forward. You let go of the pedestal and stand on both feet.

Stolzel laughs. "Of course! Of course you're from elf wasteland! Only they could breed a necromancer with their black magic." The wave dragon screams again. The entire tower rattles. It's coming closer. Stolzel says, "How fitting the moons are seeing to it that I kill the last of you myself!"

"Weak little bard," you say. "Give me my amulet!" You charge. Outside the wave dragon fans out its wings. It arches its head near the window, drawing in breath. It's preparing to roar. You rush Stolzel and kick him square in the chest, the blade of your heel stabbing into his ribs. With one foot stuck, you swing the other up.

In one motion you kick away his violin and slice your heel straight up the middle of his face. The crown catches on your foot and as you kick off of Stolzel, he stumbles back. He breaks clean through the brass railing and falls out of his tower, straight through the wave dragon's mouth as it lurches forward. The creature dissipates into a cloud of smoke and ash. You land hard against the floor.

"Mornia!" I say, stumbling forward.

"It's okay," you whisper. "I'm okay. I can feel it." You curl into a little ball and pluck Stolzel's crown off your heel. Holding it over your head, you smile. "The amulet," you say, putting the crown on your head. "It's one of these claws."

"My queen," I half joke as you adjust the crown. I crawl and collapse at your side. If I had it in me I may have gone as far as to bow or even salute you. Instead I simply ask, "Is that it then?"

The green of your eyes is more vibrant, practically glowing. "Oh yes," you say as the burns and blisters on your face fade into fresh skin. You reach for me, touching my elbow. I jolt as a warmth ripples through me. I feel a tingling as my cuts close in on themselves. It becomes easier to breathe. After a moment I think I have the strength to stand.

"King Stolzel!" a group of scattered voices calls from outside. I roll and stumble to my feet. Far, far below us, some soldiers have gathered around Stolzel's body and are looking down at him. One of them picks up the pieces of his shattered violin and they all at once look up the tower. They see us. "For the king!" one of them yells as they rush into the palace.

"I don't think we have long," I say, helping you to your feet.

You close your eyes and after a moment say, "There's nothing dead in the palace. Nowhere."

"You can feel that?"

"I can feel everything," you say. "Just hold them off. I'll bring us reinforcements."

When I look back down to the street, more soldiers are storming into the building. All around them the battle rages on. You join me at the ledge, looking over the destruction of Dromn. Between the orcs and soldiers, the fighting continues everywhere. You raise your hands like the conductor of a symphony, and the warmth healing my wounds is replaced with a chill. Everywhere, for as far as I can see, little green lights beginning appearing. They spread through the battle, through the fires, through every ruined street of the city. The eyes of the dead glow from your power. It spreads all the way to the horizon. You raise your hands even higher, and the corpses of every human, every orc, every dead animal and insect rises. And as you wave your arms each and every one of them attacks. Throughout all of Dromn, human and orc soldiers alike recoil in horror.

I turn to start looking for a weapon but a noise from outside makes me pause. From far below the balcony I hear singing. I look down to the street and Stolzel's body is standing, belting out lyrics in some language I've never heard. He cocks his head back and his eyes glow like the rest of the dead. "You're controlling the king?" I ask, but you don't answer. The ground outside the palace rumbles and three wave dragons emerge from rubble. All three take flight. All three begin roaring at the city, toppling buildings and destroying living and dead soldiers alike. You smile. Your eyes are shut and you're moving your arms and fingers in every direction while slowly swaying your hips. Somehow I know you can see it all.

From the tower's stairwell I hear a soldier's voice call out, "Up there! Up there! Go! Go!"

I turn around and charge for the entrance. When the first soldier enters I leap into the air and crush his chest with both of my knees. He falls against the wall and I rip his sword from his hand. The flash of a blade closes in at my side but I manage to duck under it. I slice off the soldier's arm and claim his sword from the falling stump. I kick him back, knocking several soldiers down the stairs behind him. More men pour in and I do my best to fend them off. My attacks are clumsy and wild. However you healed me with that amulet it didn't do anything for my fatigue. The soldiers are able to parry my attacks and even give me a few fresh cuts. They begin crowding into the room, and I do my best to hold them back. I injure several, block the attacks of a few, and then kill one.

No sooner than I draw my blade from his body does he turn on his comrades, eyes glowing green. Suddenly there are two of us fighting the soldiers, and then three and four. More keep piling into the room and with your dead minions we continue slaughtering them off. But somehow it isn't enough. They just keep coming, continuing to push themselves into the tower.

I turn to the balcony. Beyond you I see several boulders flying through the air, straight at the palace. One of the wave dragons roars the first into rubble. Another smashes straight through another wave dragon and crashes into the tower.

The entire room shakes. There's a loud creaking, the screams of soldiers, and suddenly the tower drops a few inches and tilts. You stumble toward the same ledge Stolzel fell from. I run. I leap. You start to fall, but I slide across the balcony and catch you by the wrist. I scream as I cling between you and one of the brass pipes.

"Don't let go," you say back, plainly. Your voice is distant, calm. Your eyes are barely open.

I start to lift you but out the corner of my eye I see a soldier running for me. He raises his sword and I awkwardly kick at him for all the good it'll do. He swings down at me, and for the briefest second I know it's all over. But then he's thrown forward, flying straight over us and down to the pavement below. One of your dead warriors had shoved him over the ledge. I look to it, thinking it'll help us up but instead it turns and continues in the fight.

"I can't lift you on my own, Mornia!" I yell over the carnage.

"I…" you say. "I…"

I look down and you're hanging limply. "Mornia?" I scream. When I look back into the tower, your soldiers are still fighting strong. When I look out into the city, the carnage continues. The wave dragons continue to rip apart the armies. Every soldier killed turns to face their brothers. The green glow spreads thicker, brighter. All throughout the horizon are areas so thick with the dead that they appear as green, glowing lakes.

Another volley from the catapults launches our way.

I yell for you to block them but you don't respond. The boulders crash into the tower. The entire building shakes, tilts, and we slip from the balcony. I catch hold of the ledge but the tower begins to shatter and my fingers finally slip.

Then there's only the feeling of air.

I pull you closer as we fall. I look to your eyes. They're shut. As the rush of wind slips the crown off your head you make no motion to grab at it or even change your expression. I scream your name but you don't react.

All around us, the tower is crumbling to pieces. Bodies, treasures, weapons, and fragments of the palace all drop alongside us. Throughout every corner of Dromn the green light begins to fade. I look at the approaching street below and breathe.

It should end this way, I think. We've destroyed the pure kingdom, killed the king, and you've tasted unlimited power. Your victory is absolute and I helped you until the end, just like I've always sworn I would. Maybe it's right this way. I pull you closer and brace for the impact. My final moment will be of the wind, the crumbling world, and the warmth of your body against mine. Not a bad death for the murderous son of a slumlord and a four-breasted whore.

But then I feel your heartbeat against my chest. Along with it, there's something pressed between us. Against my ribs I feel a small lump. I grin. I can't help it.

I'm such a fool. I had the travel stone all along. Plummeting to the street below I cackle. For all the times we should've died tonight we may still have a tomorrow. So I hold you as tight as I can, pressing the emerald firmly between us. I look up to the sky, seeing the tower, the riches of the kingdom, screaming and dead soldiers falling alongside us. Beyond it all I see the moons. With the second I have left, I concentrate on an ocean, a cherry blossom, green hills, and a world far, far away from the one we've destroyed. I close my eyes, focus, and we-

Acknowledgements

This story would never have existed without the lovely Christina Irwin. She was the original inspiration and my motivation for taking what was supposed to be a brief story written as a text message and turning it into my first novel. Along with her lovely cover art and about the author image, I can never thank her enough.

Much gratitude also goes to Thomas Budday, who's been reading this story and evaluating it for years.

Thank you Courtney Danyel for all of your edits and corrections.

Special thanks to my parents, Jim and Joanne, and my brothers, Mike, Josh, Dan, and Chris. Just because.

Other Fiction by Keith Blenman

Available on Kindle and/or Paperback

Bartered Breath
Bonnie Before the Brain Implants
Braaaaaains
Entrees & Statistics
Roadside Attraction, Volume 1: Siren Night
Static
Tender Buttons Two: Disco Wrecklord
Warm Winter
Where Dogs Sweat

Coming Soon

Whisper (A prelude to Necromantica)
The Ferrelf Trilogy
Roadside Attraction, Volume 2: Tramp Stamp Vamp

Blogs

This Worthless Life
http://keithblenman.blogspot.com

The Keep
http://largoafis.blogspot.com

EPILOGUE:
A King of Brass

Elize couldn't see over the shoulders of giants. Twelve of them, specifically. Mama giant. Papa giant. Two brother giants. All of them together wrangling seven giant children. Even Grandma giant was there, who remained seated in the elephant cart they'd hauled her in on. Together the family lined half of Plaza Street's fourth block, dressed in their finest tattered black bear furs.

The plaza was after all the only place undesirables were welcome to watch the procession as it marched from the city to the Folding Rock Mountains. That is unless they wished to watch from outside the city. But who could ever afford the toll back in? Certainly not a little orphan such as her.

"Excuse me?" Elize said to the backs of giants. "Excuse me! None of us can see." She felt it was only fair to include everyone. The entire plaza was packed with her countrymen, all of whom had gathered to watch the final passing of their hero, Li Ras'Brooth. Until three days prior he'd been the admiral's son. The entire kingdom knew him as Fang Breaker, who lead the charge against the serpent dragons at Luthro Marsh. It was Li who stopped the Hyokian Invasion. Li who saved the dwarf prince of Ara. And Li who was betrothed to wed the fair maiden Ursy, whom Elize and all the other girls envied and hated. He was a rare man, an unequaled man, and until three days ago the pride of the kingdom. Now he'd become a legend. And these giants were blocking Elize's only chance to say good-bye.

"Excuse me?" she said again, yelling this time but still not receiving any hint of response. She began to wonder if they could even hear her, them standing tall as trees while she wasn't even grown.

"Hush up, girl," an old man said from behind her. "You'd do best not to upset them. Angry giants are known to eat children when given the excuse."

Elize flipped off the hood of her cloak and scowled at the man with little green eyes. "That's illegal within the city walls and you know it!" she said. "And I'm twelve. I'm not a child so quit addressing me as one."

"At twelve you should know better than to make noise until after the bereaved have passed."

"How will I know they've passed if I can't see the casket?" Elize snapped. The man said something more but she ignored him. She returned to the giants and tried again for their attention. "Excuse me!" she said. "Down here!"

"Be quiet!" several other voices said from the crowd.

This was getting her nowhere. She'd have to find another spot. But where? With the entire city crowding the streets, standing in silence, and waiting in mourning for the procession to pass she couldn't exactly muscle her way to the front row. She had to find higher ground. And she had to find it fast.

Her answer came before she fully formed the question. At the center of the plaza stood a brass statue of Old Saint Stolzel. Elize regarded its height for a moment and decided it was nearly twice the size of the giants. His arms were raised to hold a plated bow and gilded violin. If she could work her way to the top, his elbow might make for a comfortable support. How different could this statue be from all the trees she'd climbed?

A clumsy fumble through the crowd later and Elize decided it could be a lot different. From afar it looked twice the height of the giants but up close it was – oh dear lunar gods- thrice the already terrifying height of the giants. Touching the leg, she felt it was slick. Also far too thick to wrap her arms around.

And then she heard the singing.

"No!" she said. "Not already!" As the procession passed, the people would break their silence and join in song. Just like Old Saint Stolzel when the first kingdom fell. As his city burned and the people were slaughtered by orcs, Stolzel stood at the gates of his palace and sang a hymn to welcome death. The song was so moving that three dragons heard it, swooped in, and began killing all the orcs. Although they were too late to save the kingdom and Stolzel himself, none of the orcs survived to see the sunrise. So now when the people of Fortia met death they greeted it with a song. And Elize was about to miss everything if she didn't act fast.

The statue was slick, so she needed support. Elize had taken to using a rope as a belt for her cloak. Not that she didn't have her own belt in her bunk, but the wizards at the orphanage always tied their cloaks with golden ropes. So one night while washing the laundry she'd claimed one for herself. And now it was her salvation. She fumbled to untie it and quickly threw one end around the leg of the statue. She then wrapped both ends around her wrist and tugged. It seemed sturdy enough so she put one foot on the statue. And then the other. And then she took her first step, followed by several more.

"Oy!" a gruff voice whispered from the crowd. "You there! Get off the statue!"

Elize turned to see the black and red armor of two soldiers. They were fumbling through the crowd, already in pursuit of her. One, an enormous bear of a man with a full beard, was holding a battle axe. The other was a wisp of a woman with silver hair and a bow slung over her shoulder. "Get off the statue!" the man said again.

Elize gulped a breath and made her decision. She took another step. Quickly she flicked the rope a little higher and took a few more steps.

"Someone grab that kid before she kills herself!" the man said, not bothering to whisper any more.

Elize kept moving. As quick as she could she flicked the rope and hoisted herself up the leg of the statue. It wasn't long before she felt a tug against her. Looking down, some old hag had grabbed hold of her cloak and was saying, "Get down from there. You'll hurt yourself!" Behind her the soldiers were closing in. Elize flicked the rope a little higher and took another step. With all the strength she could muster, she fought the woman until she heard a tear. Her cloak ripped away in the woman's hand and she was free again to climb.

"Get down here you brat!" the woman soldier said. "Don't make me shoot you down!"

Elize didn't listen. The crowd's singing was getting louder and she was running out of time. She kept climbing until she reached the waist. There things got a little easier. The statue featured the saint with a thick belt and buckle fashioned to show the seven moons in overlapping crescents. His shirt was welded with brass ruffles. Plenty of handholds. Elize reached out for the first ruffle and flinched back when an arrow bounced off the statue. Elize watched as it spiraled back down, straight into the woman soldier's hand, and then was immediately loaded back into her bow. "That was a warning shot!" she yelled. "The next one takes your eye!"

Elize held for a moment, staring down at the arrow pointed straight for her. From thousands of voices she could hear the song being sung in rounds.

"*Come to the light, my darlings! Come to the love of the lords!*" The song grew louder, and closer. "*Come to the love of the lords! Come to the light, my darlings!*" Elize took a long breath, staring down at the tip of the arrow. She thought of Li Ras'Brooth, and the tale of how he charged into a Hyokian camp, swatting arrows away with his sword. She asked herself if a time in his life ever came when he would turn away from a fight. And then she reached for the next handhold.

The woman soldier screamed, "Don't think I won't!"

"Stand down, Marmesk," the other soldier said. "We aren't shooting a child during the admiral's son's funeral. Not in this crowd. She has to come down eventually."

"By the moons!" another voice chimed in. Elize knew right away it was Brother Cloone, her ward, the wizard priest who kept watch over the orphans. She glanced down to see his ghost white scalp and glowing purple eyes. "Elize Percour! You get down here this instant!" Then to the soldiers he said, "You have to do something! She'll get herself killed!"

The bigger soldier shrugged. "We already tried scaring her down," he said. "Unless you expect me to climb up and get her we'll just have to wait."

"Elize!" Brother Cloone threatened. "Elize! These soldiers will take you to the Jerbaisy Desert! And if they don't, so help me I'll do it myself!"

Elize stopped paying attention. She grabbed another handhold, and then another. Little by little she made her way up Saint Stolzel's belly. When she reached his elbow she scaled his arm and rolled on top of the violin. The strings were thick steel cables, coiled tightly together. She'd grown up seeing this statue almost every day of her life and somehow she never realized the violin had actually been stringed. If the statue could move it might actually be able to play.

"Elize!" Brother Cloone yelled from the distant below. She couldn't see him from the top of the violin and didn't particularly care. She'd made it this far and there was no turning back. So the little girl grabbed hold of the cables and pulled her way to the bridge of the violin. She'd made it to Old Saint Stolzel's shoulder. Looking over the city, she laughed. She wasn't too late. Over the crowds and beyond the giants, she could see a troop of a hundred soldiers armored in black, the king's royal guard. They were followed by Li's onyx casket, gleaming with silver trim. Behind it marched Admiral Ras'Brooth and Li's younger brother, Deltia. And behind them, riding in a carriage and bowed in prayer was King Malka Kabar. He was a wizard, just like Brother Cloone, but old. Even from this far she could make out his wrinkles. Supposedly, even for wizards, he was ancient. And because he had no children the people often said that if he died it would be the Ras'Brooth family who would take the crown. Somewhere in every citizen's fantasy they'd all had hoped it would be Li in line for the throne. But three days ago that dream died when he'd been betrayed by the Elf Pet, Hachi Gatsu. Oh, how Elize hated that name. She hated that man for all he took from the kingdom. But what could she do? What could she say? Deltia Ras'Brooth already chased the Elf Pet out of the city. Five hundred soldiers were on his trail and it'd only be a matter of time before he'll be punished for his treason. That bastard, Elize thought. That evil, monstrous bastard. She couldn't wait for the town criers to announce his capture.

But today wasn't for revenge. Standing on the statue of an old saint, a protector of the kingdom, Elize stared out at all the masses. All of them, every last person in Dromn came out to honor their hero. Elize hoped more than anything that Li was looking down to see this spectacle. She hoped he was watching them all from the moons, overwhelmed by the love from the millions of souls he'd spent his life protecting. She hoped more than anything that he'd be able to hear her. So as the carriage came closer, she drew in the deepest breath she could hold. She wanted to be louder than everyone else. She wanted her voice to carry over the entire city. To her hero, the protector of Fortia, she wanted to sing. And as soon as the coffin passed she joined right in with the song. *"Come to the love of the lords! Come to the light, my darlings!"* She belted the words out as loud as her tiny voice would allow. She sang to her champion, filling every word with all the love she had for him. *"Come to the love of the lords! Come to the light, my darlings!"* Tears filled her eyes as he passed and she screamed the lyrics even louder. She sang over the entire city; all of the men, dwarves, elves, giants, lomin, ferrelfs, and all the mixed species in between. She sang over everybody in salute to a man greater than any of them. Chills radiated through her. The song filled her from head to toe. For her hero, for all of Dromn, Elize Percour laughed, wept, and sang.

Tomorrow,
a ferrelf lands in Fortia

Thousands of years from now,
The Vecris will be found.

To be continued...

Made in the USA
Middletown, DE
25 September 2016